WHAT I DO IS TABOO...4

Also by Yonder

WHAT I DO IS TABOO...4

YONDER

T.L. Rawlings is the next great author to emerge from Charm City-B'MORE. His definition of erotic has taken the book world by storm. Pure ecstasy of doing the act to wishing you was just in the room. He has captured not only your imagination, but in some cases, he is attached to your thongs. Get ready to clutch your breasts and hold tight to your weave.

The Chronicles of Lance, Part 2

By T.L. Rawlings

The Late Bell

As I'm running up to the front door of "The Mill," the nickname given to our high school by the students, I'm thinking to myself, *HOW COULD I BE SO LATE!* I wonder if I can get a late pass for having sex with a bad-ass stripper on a school night. A *FUCK* pass? Hilarious! The late bell sounds as I fly through the hallways and up to the second floor. Students' artwork flaps in the breeze as I float past packed classrooms. While zooming to class, I notice something strange. Not a soul is in the hallways, not even a hall monitor.

YES!

As I get to Dr. Clinton's classroom, I open the door just in time to hear her say, "Lance Joseph?"

"Here!" I say while panting, and amazingly, instead of asking any questions, she looks me up and down, flashes a devilish smirk, winks her eye, and replies, "Your turn, Mr. Joseph."

"Huh?" I say as my classmates chuckle and snicker.

"Your report? Your story?"

"Oh!" I reply, remembering the two-week homework assignment that I had just started and almost finished two days ago.

As I step in front of my Honors English class, all of a sudden, there is an outburst of noise. Girls are laughing and smiling. All of the dudes are throwing their hands in the air, looking away, and even running out the classroom! Except for this one dude, Lil' Antwan, who is sitting at the front of the classroom just smiling. That's when I realize I'm standing butt-ass naked! *WHAT THE FUCK!* I was so sprung that I had left without my clothes! At that moment, Dr. Clinton walks up behind me and whispers in my ear, "Are you ready, baby? I have to go." Then she licks my ear and grabs my ass.

Startled from my sleep, I woke up to Dream whispering in my ear, "Are you ready, baby? I have to go."

She was fully dressed in a black velour FILA sweat suit, with tennis shoes and a hat to match. It was morning, and as the sun shined into her crib, it looked totally different from the night before. It was still a bad place...but normal... not sexy.

"Umm, yeah...oh shit! What time is it?"

"It's 7:02, baby. I figured you had to be somewhere this morning. Where do you need me to drop you off?" she asked.

I had no clue where I was. *Stupid move!* I just knew I wasn't in Baltimore.

"If you can drop me off at the subway downtown, I'll good from there. Charles Center or Lexington, it doesn't matter," I said.

12

She leaned over and kissed me with her soft, liquid lips. Then she said, "You were good last night."

OH SHIT! Don't wake me up from this dream, Lord! I owe you!

Now since we never mentioned our ages, and I had no business being in Eldorado's Strip Joint, I didn't think it would be cool to have her drop me off at my high school. *Ya think?*

Before I could ask where my clothes were, she told me, "I threw your clothes in the wash this morning and ironed them for you."

"Really? Thank you!" I was shocked. "What time did you get up?" I asked.

"About five-thirty. I usually head to the gym early. Then come home, shower, and get some sleep before running a few errands and getting started with my day job about two o'clock."

"Day job? Where do you work?" I inquired.

"I help manage a private firm from my home office," she replied.

"Cool."

As I began to put on my pants, she told me to hold up. Dream then went to a closet and brought me a towel and washcloth.

"Take a shower, baby. You don't want to start your day smelling like hot, delicious sex!"

She busted out laughing. I had to laugh, too. I mean, damn, she had this whole thing very well thought out. Very organized. She definitely had her shit together, but I guess that's what *WOMEN* do.

I jumped in the shower, which was separate from the tub. She even had a detachable showerhead that you could use all over your body. I felt like I was in an Irish Spring commercial. *Oh snap! OIL OF OLAY?!* I had always seen the commercial, but never the soap. She had bars and body wash everywhere. Everything smelled so damn good. I wondered if I had time to jerk off, but then I realized I was already late enough.

"There's some cologne and deodorant in the first drawer on your left!" she yelled.

"Word? Thanks!"

As I dried off as quickly as possible, I looked in the mirrored medicine cabinet on the wall and saw SHE HAD EVERYTHING! Even my favorite cologne Fahrenheit! I've always been into smelling good. I felt like Slick Rick. *LaDiDaDi.*

I came out the bathroom and got dressed in a flash. Dream, who was looking through some papers, handed me a sandwich wrapped in foil.

"What's this?"

"Bacon egg and cheese on toast; you gotta eat, baby," she said.

"Thank you again. You wanna get married?" I asked, damn near serious. I didn't want to tell her that I didn't eat pork, though. *Oh well!*

We laughed on the way out.

As we walked to the garage, I saw Meeko tearing up his food!

"Alright, Meeko," I said.

He paid me no attention.

Dream drove a Black 280 ZX with cream leather interior. *Hot!* I didn't even notice the night before because I was out of it.

On our ride back into downtown Baltimore, she told me the area we were in was Silver Spring. I had heard of Silver Spring, but I had never been there. It was a nice area. We talked a little, but no real conversation. I began to realize it had been just sex, even though she tried to make it seem like she was interested in my juvenile convo. This would be another story I kept in my mental diary.

See, I was never much on bragging about the women or girls I had sex with. My mother gave me three golden rules about women and they reign true till this day. One, never call a woman out her name (bitch, ho, etc.). Two, never put your hands on a woman unless you're trying to defend yourself. And three, if you have sex with a girl and don't run her name in the dirt, you can get it again!

Betty was right on all counts! I could never understand dudes that lied on their dick. Why? Why would you claim to have had sex with a girl when you didn't? You might have finger popped her, but you didn't have intercourse! Anyway...

"Is this good?" she asked, pulling up to my destination.

"Oh, that was quick. Yeah, I'll be straight from here."

"Okay." She leaned over and gave me a wet kiss, which I reciprocated!

You're gonna remember my young ass, I thought to myself.

"Hope to see you down at the club again, Mr. Big Dick," she said while smiling.

"Yeah, yeah...I'll be down there again. What nights are you there?" I asked.

"Tuesdays, Thursdays, Saturdays, and Sundays," she replied as I got out the car.

"Cool. See you later. I had a ball."

What did I just say? A ball?

"Me, too," she said.

After I closed the door and she drove off, I yelled, "SHIT!" I never got her number! I was ready to chase her car down, but as I turned around, a boy with a book bag on his shoulder bumped into me. *Book bag! I have to get to school!* The good thing was I lived within walking distance of my school. Since they were doing renovations on our actual high school, which wasn't far from me either, they moved us to Subbrook Middle School's old building, which sat at the end of my street. *Heaven!* If I got up late, I could still make it on time. And having people come over after school? Not a problem.

As I walked up to my school, I heard the first bell. I dashed to my locker, grabbed my notebook, and ran to Dr. Clinton's class. I loved Dr. C's class. Not because I was a big fan of English, but because there were some of the finest, most intelligent, and down-to-earth young ladies in this class. Three of my favorite ladies, Carrie, Dionne, and Lisa, sat right by me in class. *Perfect.* Carrie was that homie/lover/friend type. You know, fellas! She was the total package. The homegirl who you could talk to about everything, even another girl's banging-ass body. And if given the opportunity you'd definitely fuck her! There was only one problem. She always kept a boyfriend. Some nigga who didn't even go to our school and was usually two or three years older than us. Oh, and she had another one in our school! Classic homegirl Carrie!

Then there was my girl Dionne, the brainiac closet freak. Straight A's and a phat ass! She was kind of "offish" to people, a bit anti-social to most. However, she would give Carrie and I the goods every week on her sexual exploits and even show us Polaroid photos as proof! Dionne was also a scary flirt. Scary because this sistah would follow through on her flirts, but then all of her girlfriends mysteriously knew the next school day. *Never trust a big butt and a smile... POISON!* But she was cool.

And last but not least, Lisa Hamm, who was the girl that most teen romantic comedy movies were centered around. Kind of quiet, pretty, nice figure, cheerleader, played volleyball, SGA President, on the Honor Roll...and for some reason, we were friends even though some other guys didn't pay her a lot of attention. *Go figure.* I enjoyed our conversations, and I think it surprised her that I was intelligent even though I loved to party and have fun. Lisa Hamm would turn out to be the young lady who would change my life. You'll get that part later in the story.

No matter how tired I was, I always felt a little rejuvenated when I got to school. That was the case today more than ever because...well shit, last night's events and breakfast this morning...I felt like a grown-ass man! Until I realized where I was, which was in school.

"Everyone, please pass up your homework assignments to the front," Dr. Clinton said.

FUCK! I hate when I do that. But I can't lie. I get an adrenaline rush from doing a paper or assignment at the last minute.

"Now what were you doing last night that you didn't do...and you smell good as shit! I love when a dude smells good. What's that?" Carrie whispered.

I had to laugh at her crazy ass. "Fahrenheit."

"He always smells good," Dionne interjected.

"Thank you, D," I said.

"You just need to stop being a fucking tease all your life," Dionne added with a wicked smirk.

Immediately, we busted out into spurts of muffled laughter, which drew Dr. Clinton's attention.

"Alright, y'all," Dr. Clinton warned as she peered over her glasses. She knew when we were about to get rowdy, and after we got started, a dominoes affect would roll through the classroom.

"I'm saying, Lance, I know you probably have a big dick. At least that's the rumor."

"Hold up, D!" I laughed the words and pulled Dionne closer. "First off, stop being so fucking loud, and two, who's talking about me and my dick?"

By now, Carrie was in tears laughing and other people in the class were trying to figure out what was so juicy about our conversation.

Dionne continued, "Nigga, you know you packing. So when are you gonna give me some?"

"Girl, you're full of shit. You're the biggest tease-freak there is. You don't want none!"

"Whateva," Dionne responded, looking as if she was ready to challenge me right in the class. "Boy, I back up everything I say. You've seen the pictures!"

Once again, we tried our hardest to laugh in whispered muffles.

"Exactly! The dude with the dick half way down his thigh! Ole' thigh dick having muthafucka! And you said you loved fucking him. NOT! He didn't hurt the pussy; he KILLED it. YOU LOVED FUCKING HIM?! I'm not messing with you, D!"

Carrie added, "I know that's right. D, you're a fucking low pro ho! You the truth, shorty!"

By now, I was laughing so hard that I was crying. That's why these were my girls!

While we were deep in our sexually explicit NC-17 discussion, Lisa Hamm was listening while reading our class assignment and getting every bit of it. She just smiled and shook her head. Even though she had beautiful, dark chocolate skin, I could tell she was blushing from time to time. That's what intrigued me about her. Lisa was no prude, even though her parents were well off and she was stupid-Intelligent. She was extremely cool.

"How do y'all get any work done? Y'all are trippin'," Lisa scolded while laughing.

"I know," I said in my own defense. "I'm trying to get A's like you. These ladies are bad influences."

"Right. You love every minute of it!" Lisa said.

"Yes, he does!" Carrie added her two cents.

"And he'd really love it if he let me come over. We know you're right down the street," Dionne said as if she had serious incriminating evidence on me.

"D, that's why I keep away from you, because my shit would be in the school newspaper the next day."

"Whateva! Anyway, Carrie, stop acting like you don't be getting yours on the weekends with them older guys you be messing with." Dionne turned her attack to Carrie.

"Me?" Carrie said, surprised.

"Yeah, you hoochie!" Dionne said.

This time, all four of us burst out laughing. We didn't even try to contain it. I saw Dr. Clinton look up and start to get out of her chair.

Before she could reprimand us, I said, "I apologize, Dr. Clinton. They were laughing at me because they didn't believe a guy like me writes poetry."

"Really, Mr. Joseph? Now why wouldn't they believe that? He really is a wonderful writer. As a matter of fact, since you have so much to say today, why not entertain the whole class?" Dr. Clinton replied.

"Naw, I'm alright, Doc!" I tried to weasel my way out.

"No, I insist, really!" Dr. Clinton said in a stern tone.

"Okay," I responded, knowing there was no way out of it.

I grabbed my composition book and walked to the front of the classroom. All eyes were on me as I fumbled through my journal. I felt sweat rolling down my eyebrow. As I looked around the class, I saw everyone's body language. Guys were squirming while waiting for the bell to ring, and the girls were always paying attention. Even when it seemed like they weren't, they were listening. I looked over to my crew in the corner. Dionne, Carrie, and Lisa had their arms folded and their necks cocked, just waiting for me to fuck up so they could get on me later.

I looked over at Lisa and remembered I had a poem that I had just written about her. This was a golden opportunity, so...

"Okay, this poem is called "When".

"What did you win?" Earl Jenkins yelled out from the back of the classroom.

He's an asshole!

Ignoring him, I started reciting.

I remember daily moments
But
Never the exact time
When
I met the one I wanted to be mine
When
It made perfect sense for the sun to shine
When
She became the verse to my rhyme
When
She became my center of attention
When
She was the crush I couldn't mention

"Awww shucks!" Mary Stuart blurted.

The class started getting into the poem, seeing if they could figure out if it was someone they knew. Some of them were laughing, but all were paying attention. I felt myself warming up and getting loose as I continued.

See
We're from different worlds and I understand
How
Wrong it may seem if I was her man
How
Our friends would react if I held her hand
How
Many questions would arise if I made a stand and said
How
I really feel about her
My day doesn't start without her
On my mind
So
Until that time
When

And like a perfect scene from a movie, the bell rang! And the class went crazy! People were clapping, high-fiving me as they left the room, and giving me props. As we walked into the hallway, there were people outside the room who said they heard the commotion. Now it was going around the school that I was a poet. *Perfect!*

Carrie and Dionne were leaning against the lockers with their arms still folded.

"Okay...you got skills. You got skills," Carrie said as she patted me on the back.

"Edgar Allan Poe...Langston Hughes...had the ladies all wet and juicy, especially Lisa," Dionne commented.

"Huh? What? What did she say? Where is she?"

"Calm down, nigga! She didn't have to say anything. She was sitting there all dreamy eyed, and then it looked like she was about to cry! Whateva...you were alright."

Dionne could be a hater at times, but more importantly, I had just realized Lisa was into poetry...and best of all, my poetry. Now I was looking forward to seeing her again.

After my oratory debut, it felt like the rest of the day flew by. While I loved high school, I really enjoyed my after-school activities. And, believe it or not, I really enjoyed my after-school job. Sure, it was just a burger joint, but what made this Mickey D's different from the others was that it was rated the second highest volume moneymaker and the highest quality store in all of Baltimore. We were the Beverly Hills of burger joints!

My coworkers were from all over the city, but together we made a great team. The owner gave us our own bank accounts with direct deposit, and the hottest uniforms the Mickey D's catalog had to offer. Okay, it wasn't just the money. It was my fine-ass female coworkers in them tight-ass, burger-flipping, "can-I-help-you-please" pants!

One girl in particular—well, lady being that she was twenty-four—became my greatest sexual sensei. Her name was Shawntel...no last name needed. Shawntel was a shorty, literally. She stood about 5'1" but was about 130 pounds of Lawd Have Mercy! She had a caramel complexion, short Anita Baker haircut, and slanted eyes. Her full, luscious, sexy lips were reminiscent of Millie Jackson, Chaka Khan, or a Rolling Stones' album cover. Even though a pair of nice tits is wonderful to behold, I am truly an ass man. So, the fact that Shawntel hardly had any titties was truly overshadowed by her glorious ass! You could sit a lunch tray on her ass and have her jog around the block and nothing would spill. Shawntel was the quiet type, and her daily flirtation with me was very cute and sneaky. I was definitely attracted to her.

The only thing is Shawntel was the cousin of one of the managers. No biggie for me, because like my mother told me, "Don't fuck and tell." (Well, she said that in so many words.)

I always enjoyed working with Shawntel. It seemed like she always had a flirtatious sexual one-liner for any comment I made to her. One day, we finally had to close the store together. I was cleaning the grill, while Shawntel was cleaning the food stations in the front of the store. Every time she came back to my area she would slide in an innuendo.

"A man that can do the dishes? Mmmm mmmm, that's sexy," she said in her sweet voice.

"A woman that can walk like you? Mmmm mmmm mmmm!" I replied.

We both laughed, but neither of us were about to back down as we got closer to each other. I wiped my hands off on my apron.

"I must say, girl, you are very attractive. Really."

"So are you. How old are you again? Sixteen? So young," she commented with a laugh.

"I know, but at least I'll be around after your old ass croaks!"

"Oooooooohh, you're Mr. Funnyman. I got you. Don't make me fuck you up back here."

"You mean fuck me down, with your short ass."

"Ooooh, no you didn't! You're crazy!"

We both were laughing so hard and joking around that we forgot we were in the back of a burger joint. Shawntel took her hat off and walked to the break room right in the middle of our conversation. She got to the doorway and summoned me to follow her with her cute little finger. When I got to the doorway, she was standing in it not moving. She was smiling, but had a seductive look in her eyes. Believe me, I knew (and still know) that look.

"What, girl?" I asked. "You're not gonna let me in?"

Shawntel backed up one step and said, "You can come...in."

As I walked in the door, she stepped to me and pressed her soft body against me. I leaned down into the wettest, hottest kiss I had ever experienced. My dick was about to burst through my cheap-ass polyester work pants. She was on her tippy toes and didn't back off one bit. This was erotic beyond kissing. We moved around the small room like we were in a scene from *Fatal Attraction*.

Amazingly enough, I stopped and whispered, "Girl, we're at work. You're sneaky as hell!"

"So, okay, when can I come see you?" she asked. "What are you doing after this? Are your parents home?"

Still a little in awe, I replied, "Oh, it doesn't matter. My pops is cool. He's probably not home anyway. My boy is coming to pick me up, so you can roll with me."

"Cool. I'll just catch a cab home from your house."

"Actually, I live by Milford Mill subway station," I said.

"Perfect! I live by West Cold Spring station! That's even better. Let's finish up so we can roll," she said, then kissed me again, put her hat on, and walked out the break room.

DAAAMN! Her little ass is the truth! Well...little woman with a fat ass!

I was glad the manager didn't walk in, but they usually never came out of the office while counting money.

Even though I was excited as all get-out that Shawntel was coming over, I'd learned from dating schoolgirls to never assume that SEX will happen. No matter how much foreplay, kissing, sucking and finger-popping you do, it doesn't mean she's going to let you get some. And I was cool with that. I'd even shocked some young ladies in the past that had damn near got naked and wanted to stop. I would simply tell them okay and start putting my clothes back on. I wasn't catching any rape charges! My moms said, "If a girl says stop, YOU STOP! You don't want to go to jail over getting some!" I couldn't agree more. One girl even begged me to come back and have sex with her after she saw I was putting my clothes back on with the quickness. I was pissed at her. I don't play games with sex, and since Shawntel was so quiet, I figured this might be a night of hot foreplay. Still, I was cool with that.

Before I knew it, we were done closing the store and waiting for my man Ryan to pick us up. Ryan and I had been friends since elementary school. He was one of those friends who I bullshit in school with; we also played sports together. But we never talked about our sexual exploits or who we were dating. So, when Ryan picked me up and saw I was bringing a fine-ass female with me to my house, he seemed a little shocked.

"What's up, man?" I said.

"What's up, L?" Ryan replied.

"Hey, Ryan. This is my friend Shawntel."

"Hello, Shawntel."

"Hello," she responded.

"Do you mind if she rides with us to my house?"

"Come on, man. Why would you even ask that? Any friend of yours is a friend of mine," Ryan said while laughing

"Yeah, whateva, nigga!" I had to laugh, too.

Ryan's parents were pretty well off and had several cars. So, it was cool that he was able to pick us up in their Mazda 929 with the leather interior. A very comfortable ride. We talked about random stuff and laughed as we rode about twelve minutes to my house. Every now and then Ryan would give me a nod as if to say, *You better tear that pussy up!*

As we pulled up to my townhouse, I gave Ryan a pound and said, "Thanks, man. I'll see you tomorrow."

"Oh, for sure, you will definitely see me tomorrow." Ryan nodded and stared at me with big eyes. "Nice meeting you, Shawntel."

"Nice meeting you, as well, Ryan."

I quickly jumped from the passenger seat and opened the door for Shawntel. As she got out, I saw Ryan look back at her ass. Then he looked to me and mouthed, *DAAAAMMMNN!* I just laughed, shook my head, and closed the door.

"Your neighborhood is so quiet. Does everyone go to sleep at eleven o'clock?"

I laughed. "Naw, but I guess it is kind of quiet. I like it, though."

Since I didn't see my father's car, I knew we could go right upstairs. As we walked in, I turned on the living room lights and said, "This is the grand tour!"

We both laughed.

"This is nice and comfortable," Shawntel said.

"I'll take your coat. You can have a seat or we can go upstairs?"

"I'm following you," she replied.

I quickly hung her coat in our packed closet. *All these old fucking coats!* Then I led her upstairs. My parents' room had the big TV, so since Pop wasn't home and probably wouldn't be home for a while, I led her into there.

Shawntel took off her shoes and asked to use the bathroom. While she was in the bathroom, I flipped through the channels and turned the volume down a little so I could hear if my father came home early. He had some of the loudest keys in the world!

As Shawntel came out of the bathroom, she asked, "Where can I put my bag and purse?"

"I'll put them in my room."

When I returned, she was stretched out on the bed on her stomach, with her head at the foot of the bed watching TV. I sat on the floor at the foot of the bed and leaned back on the bed.

"So where are your parents?" she asked.

"My father works at a lounge with his girlfriend at night. So, he gets in around...well...actually, I'm usually sleep when he gets home. And my mother lives down near Camden Yards. They've been separated about two years. What about your parents? Are they together?"

"Yeah. They live in Edmondson Village. That's where I grew up. But now I live with my cousin Shirley over near Coldspring Lane."

It was a cool conversation...small talk. Really we couldn't have given a flying fuck about anything we just said except for my father not coming home for a while. As most guys, I was just trying to figure out when to...

"Come here," Shawntel told me.

When I turned my head, she leaned toward me, and we shared a long, deep, luscious kiss that drowned out all sounds. We instantly forgot what we were talking about and remembered why we're here.

She lay back on the bed, and I crawled on top of her. We continued to kiss passionately, as I thrust, twirled, and pumped my hips as if I was already inside her. She moaned softly. I began to feel on her breasts through her clothes, and she loved it.

Now for the test. This is where I can see if this young woman is comfortable with me for real!

As I licked and nibbled on her neck ever so gently, I attempted to slide my hand down her pants. Since we had changed clothes before we left work, she was now wearing a pair of tight designer jeans. I played with her bellybutton, and she giggled. I then lifted her shirt and bra and began sucking and licking on her titties. I couldn't resist nibbling her plump, juicy nipples. Shawntel started to grind her hips and threw her head back. Now my impossible mission was to kiss, suck, and undo her jeans while not fucking up the flow we had going. I fought to remain calm so I wouldn't bust a nut in my pants because she was so sexy! I finally got her bra undo for full access to her beautiful breasts. I was still trying to unbutton the top button on her jeans, though. Then I finally said in my head, *Fuck it,* and went for her zipper.

"Stop...stop. Let's go to your room," she panted.

"Okay."

I turn off the TV, and we laughed while walking in the dark to my room across the hall. I opened my curtains, allowing the moonlight to shine in. I heard her close the door. When I turned around, she was pulling off her pants, panties, and shirt. Then she dropped her bra on the floor. My shock didn't stop me from quickly stripping down. I'm far from bashful when it's time to get naked!

Now, even though Dream sucked my dick, I learned quickly not to assume that Shawntel would.

Once she saw my dick hard, all she said was, "Do you have a condom?"

Jumping up, I opened my top dresser drawer and grabbed a condom. No time to fumble with the condom, I took my time making sure it was on the right side. I looked at Shawntel on the bed; her body was amazing. As I climbed on top of her, she immediately grabbed my dick and put it inside her.

"Oh shit...ohhh...shit...yes, Lance..."

I began to stroke and tried to think about anything but how good her pussy felt on my dick. I could feel her squeezing me inside her. It felt wonderful. I just didn't want to cum too fast. But I began to realize there was another distraction helping me not to cum.

"Fuck me! Fuck me! Take this pussy! Shit...shit...shit! Oooooh! Ooooohhh fuck! Yes, Lance!" Shawntel yelled as my new wooden headboard banged up against the wall.

It was about 12:30 a.m. on a school night, and Shawntel was right. I lived in a very quiet neighborhood. I was beginning to realize just how quiet it was.

"Work this pussy! Fuck me, baby! Yes...take it! Take it... this wet pussy..."

Now let me explain my dilemma. I grew up in a townhouse, connected houses for those who don't know. Being that the

Brookview community was a new modernized development, the walls were thin. Thin enough for my neighbor Danielle and I to be able to knock "hello" to one another on the wall and hear it. If her music was loud, I could hear it and vice versa. Feel me? Danielle and I were not only neighbors, we went to the same school, were in the same grade, and had some of the same classes. She had a twin brother that I hung with sometimes, too. So, on a school night at 12:30 a.m. the X-rated show that I was now a part of was on full blast. I was in total shock.

"What? What's wrong, baby? Why are stopping? Did you cum?" Shawntel asked.

"Ummm...I'm just..." I tried to come up with words.

"What? What's wrong?"

"I'm just tripping because you were so quiet at work and..."

"So! Lance, come on, don't stop, baby. Come on."

Shawntel commenced to turning over and getting on all fours. Her ass was beautiful! Plump and soft. I just couldn't resist it. And even though I imagined Danielle with her ear pressed against the wall and calling her girlfriends on three-way, I dove back in.

"That's right, baby! Give me that good dick. Shit. Smack my ass! Smack my ass, baby!"

I indulged her every pleasure. At first, I smacked her ass like a baby. Then when I realized she wanted more, I went harder until my hand hurt and she was bouncing back on my dick like I was rubber.

"Hold up...hold up. Shhhh," I whispered.

"What, your father? What, baby?"

I really thought I heard someone in the house, even keys. But, it was nothing. I opened the door to double check, though. Sweating and a little dizzy, I came back in the room and locked the door. Shawntel was lying under the covers.

"Is he here?" she asked.

"No...I must..."

Before I could get it out, she threw off the covers and said, "Lay down on your back, baby. Did you cum yet?"

"No. My dick got soft in the commotion," I replied, trying to be funny, but she was about her business.

Shawntel went in my drawer and got another condom. She then got on the bed and rolled off the old condom. Then she started jerking me off while spitting on my dick. It felt so good. I was trying to relax so I could get hard again. She stroked me slow and long. I was soooo glad her hands were not dry! That's the worst. Always moisten your hands for a hand-job, ladies. That's a PSA, Penis Service Announcement.

Up and at 'em! I was ready. Shawntel slid the condom on and then slid down on my manhood. She placed her petite hands on my chest and arched her back. After about three strokes, she began again.

"Ohhh shit...you have some good dick, baby! I love this dick, baby! Is this pussy good, baby? You're in this pussy deep, nigga! Fuuuuuuuccckkk me! Fuck...shit! Yes, yes, YES!"

It felt extremely good, and now I was tingling up my spine. I began to pump from the bottom. This made Shawntel lay on me so she could start sucking on my ear and neck while still pumping. She began to claw into my chest. It hurt like shit, but instead of stopping, I just pumped harder. We were both screaming now, and then...

"Ooooohh shit, Shawntel! I'm about to cuuu..." I groaned

"Yes, baby! Cum for me baby! AhhhhOOOHhh, I'm cumming!" she yelled.

We shook and grabbed each other like we were on the edge of a building. Then we fell...about thirteen stories... onto my bed.

The bed was drenched, but I was too tired to care. That was straight ridiculous. Shawntel had just taught me a valuable lesson. Never underestimate a quiet girl.

She rolled over and began rubbing my chest. Then she laughed.

"Why did you keep stopping?" she asked.

"Girl, you surprised the hell out of me."

We laughed, caressed each other, and then fell into a deep sleep...right there.

The End

Letter to My Readers...

What I Do Is Taboo is a Book of Completion. That's why it's a seven-book series. Seven is completion in the Bible. When the series is complete, you will see tremendous growth in all the characters, especially spiritually. The growth will be emotionally and just better decision making for all involved. When Taboo is complete, you will actually understand why Mr. Roarke became who he is, why Maggie is mad, and also the influences that started Henson Phillip, III. Enjoy the ride until book seven. Then, you can get off the roller coaster of life. But, wait...then you have to make the right decision in your own life.

YONDER
AKA MR. TABOO
AKA MR. ROARKE

A Bowl of Fruit

I never knew
How exotic a bowl
Of fruit could be
A banana used
As a penis
Plums acting
As balls
A mouth as
The teacher
A bowl of fruit

Henson's Story

It's Monday morning, and I don't have the typical Monday blues. My ride in was smooth, but so was my weekend. The weather didn't appear to want to cooperate with my suede jacket, so I decided to skip the Metro. It seems the parking gods had guarded and saved my favorite spot for me right next to a candy-apple-red drop-top Benz coupe. The executive who drove it was from old money, no doubt. There was even a building named after her family in Georgetown.

"A conquest for another day," I said out loud.

I filled my lungs with the smell of the city—bus exhaust, bullshit, politicking, and hustling.

"Henson Phillip, The Third has arrived back to work."

I did my usual morning thing, grabbing one of the four copies of the *Wall Street Journal* that were located in front of my office suite. I did my customary wink to the receptionist. She dishes the dirt on everyone, but she's in my pocket enough not to dish any dirt on me. I can hear my mom's voice in my head almost as clear as the Chuck Brown playing on my Bose system.

Ignore them fast-ass young gals, Henson! They'll get you in trouble.

I like trouble, though.

Upon arriving at my cubicle, I notice flowers on my desk, and not just a few. After counting them, I found there were five dozen yellow, pink, and red roses. I stepped back out of my cubicle to check the nameplate.

Henson Phillip, III. That's me.

I looked around again. My whole cubicle was full of the floral arrangements. It looked like Minnesota Avenue's florist shop.

I'm not dead, so what is this about?

I went looking for my co-worker, Crystal, to see if she could shed some light on this. I finally found her. Crystal stood 5'4" and had a winning hand with her *Brickhouse* measurements of 36-24-36, whether au natural or store bought.

Smiling like she had won the Powerball, she ran to me and asked, "Did you like them?"

"What are you talking about?" I replied.

"The flowers!"

I said, "What's the occasion?"

PAUSE:

She is rewarding me for having sex with her over the weekend. This is crazy, getting rewarded for being good in bed. But, I like it.

BACK TO STORY (BTS):

"So, do you like them?"

I again said, "What's the occasion?"

She stepped closer to me and responded, "Henson, you opened up a part of me that has been hidden. Your willingness to control me brought out my inhibitions, and I loved it. Ever since I was a little girl, because I look like a Barbie doll, folks have always let me control them. Most people treat me like a prima donna, which I can't stand. But you—my god—you Henson, just took control of me, and I loved it."

REECTION:

Fellas, women who have control really don't want it. More than likely, strong, single mothers raised them, and these women take on the same characteristics.

BTS:

So, I sat there dumbfounded because this girl had bought me all these flowers. Then, Devin, my alter ego, started speaking to me. *Henson, that's right. They are giving us flowers now because, as I told you over the weekend, I would take care of us, and I did by taking control of that situation this weekend. We're legends at this job. We can do anything. We're going to own this building.*

Crystal returned to her desk, but before she left, she told me that she would meet me for lunch. I mustered up a smile and reluctantly replied, "Okay."

So, I am at my desk feeling myself, but trying not to act too conceited. Just last Friday I was a regular "Joe" at the office. Now it's Monday, and I've been catapulted to a local celebrity at in the office.

"Morning, Phillip."

The words spilled into my cubicle, and I could only imagine the strange look on Mr. Gotta Know Everything's face.

"Perry," I bellowed back in my Walter Cronkite voice while quickly shuffling papers to appear busy.

After all, it was Monday, and I needed one of those red Staples "Easy" buttons so I could have a door, and not bluish grey fabric-trimmed office dividers.

I've got to get back in the government.

I tried my hand in the private sector, but the economy was on a roller coaster ride with no intentions of slowing down.

While sitting at my desk, I started fantasizing about the wonderful weekend I had. Me, Henson Phillip, III, had finally busted a nut in a woman and came on three other women's faces. *I am a bad man,* I thought

Then Devin kicked in, sounding like KITT from the old 80's show, *Knight Rider. No, Henson, I'm a bad man.*

Ask me how productive I was after that thought. As the day passed, I began wondering what was next for me sexually, but I am still kind of scared. They say there's a freak threshold you don't want to cross, because if you do, there's no returning to ordinary intercourse. I think I crossed it in my twenties, and I shudder at the thought of my wife-to-be being a boring lover.

Lunchtime finally came, and I was suddenly overtaken with the urge to avoid Crystal. So, I went to the men's restroom and planned to go down the back stairs instead of using the elevator. I handled my business, washed my hands, smoothed my waves and goatee, and just as I was about to leave the bathroom, Crystal bolted in, shocking the hell out of me. My mouth was open so wide you could have seen what was left of my breakfast oatmeal in my stomach.

"Henson, I'm ready right now," she stated. Then she backed me into a stall.

Half wanting this and half waiting on the crew of a reality show to burst in, I frantically questioned, "What are you doing?"

She replied, "You will be my lunch today."

While pushing her and trying to get out of the stall, Devin kicked in again, dropping our pants and making me stand on the commode. With dick in one hand, he used the other hand to brace himself with the door and then shoved my dick in her mouth. I think the head hit the back of her neck.

I am loving every minute of it.

PAUSE:

What the hell am I doing getting my dick sucked in the bathroom at work? And by a white girl at that!

BTS:

Devin starts trying to choke her with the dick. I think it's hitting her tonsils. She's taking it and loving it, though. Now, I turn her around, close the lid on the commode, and tell her to get on her knees. Then I start shoving it in her so hard that I'm hurting myself. While maintaining my balance on the stall's slippery veneer and smiling to myself, I thank myself for not wearing my suede shoes that match my jacket.

This time in a video game Mortal Combat voice, Devin booms, *Finish her!*

I start counting in my head, and when I get to 110, I prepare to release my massive load of cum. She's screaming with her face smashed against the stall's wall, and I'm screaming right along with her. Devin didn't give a damn where we were. Then, it happened. Someone walked into the bathroom.

Phillip, is that you?

The End

I would like to introduce to the world someone I consider my lil' sister. Her gift is tremendous, and I'm happy to have her first published piece in my book.

Can You Half Love Me?

Give me passion in fractions
And peace in season, truth in sample
And riddles instead of reason
Compliments in temporary intervals

Oh, insult my intelligence; better yet, my intuition
Will you confuse and keep me bemused?
Wondering who you really are
Where you are when you say you're only ten minutes
  away
And who she, or damn it, he might be to you
Or explain to me why this receipt
Has the necklace you gave me times three

Can you explain this cheap, faded earring?
Or this dumb-ass fake nail I stepped on and hair on
  my pillow?
Or how about the corner of that gold wrapper on the
  floor? Apparently you couldn't find it in the dark
When I let you hit dat raw
Or get mad at me because someone said hi to me at
  the bar When you were over there actin' like you
  knew that chick When I saw you slippin' her your
  card

47

Can you half love me like my ex?
Show him you can do it better
And make me think we have a chance at bliss, baby
    booties, and onesies instead of the typical
    predictable dumb shit, like you got me vexed with
    new shit
Not after-club numbers on flyers and floozy
    goodnight
Or *Where you at, baby* texts disturbing my beauty
    rest
Oh, baby, please give me that cinnamon-sprinkled
    honey-sugar sweet-split love in two fourth
That way, if you give me more---umm a half
I'll know I'm special; you shared and splintered man
Half love me the best you can!

~Ye'Wande' Sherise

Maggie's Madness

Mirror to My Soul

Toys, Sex, and Orgasms
Have been my friends for so long

Going cold-turkey
Is not an option

Fulfillment and enjoyment
Is why I live

Shaking legs
Toes constantly at attention

Sweat rolling off my forehead
My cornrows get tight

Damn! It's another
O

BTS:

The problem with being married is that it's a box that doesn't allow me to be me. I need to grow up or else I think I am lacking at home will eventually destroy the good love, good husband, good children, and good life that I actually already have.

I am Maggie, the diva that inspired Maggie's Madness.

The only reason I think I do all the mischief I do is because I am searching for love or approval from all the wrong people. At least that's what I came up with from listening to daytime talk shows. It stems from watching my mother and grandma during my childhood. They did everything for money in order to pay the bills and take care of us kids. I had a lot of uncles and misters coming through our Section 8 housing.

However, my family is upper middle class, so I actually don't need a dime. I have naturally fallen into the same pattern as my role model mommy dear, though. I have sex with strangers for no reason–maybe just to feel the closeness. I am also a people pleaser. It's on my resume!

It's never about me. I like to drive men and women crazy. That's why what Maggie does is taboo. Should I just surrender and be a good housewife, mother, and student? Or should I surrender, go "hoe-wild", and go back to sleeping with everybody again? Let me not talk and just pray:

Dear God,

It's me, Maggie. I need you to grant me this one thing. Take this need to be close to other men away from me. In Jesus' name I pray. Amen.

I finally finished my paper for Professor Kindred, which I made all neat. After arriving at the college, instead of doing my presentation in the class, I go straight to the professor's office and knock on the door.

"Come in!" he yelled.

I entered, and he greeted me.

"Margaret, it's so good to see you."

PAUSE:

When he calls me Margaret, it makes me feel like a little girl. Only my mother and grandmother call me that. BTS:

This is something that's been haunting me. Getting my degree is the accomplishment that has escaped my grip for too long. At Ballou Senior High School, I thought I would go straight to college, such as Hampton or Howard A&T. Attending an Ivy League college never occurred to me. Finally, after marriage and children, here I am in the Arts and Sciences building.

My husband had told me, "Honey, you are enough. We have enough. You don't have to put yourself through this with school."

"It's a personal dream I let defer. I have to do it for me," *had been* my reply.

"Good day, Professor."

He replied, "You must have something good for me. You have that anxious look on your face, Margaret."

"Yes, Professor. This is not only my best work. This is most likely the best paper you will ever get at this university."

"Well, Margaret," he interrupted, "you will have to beat out some of my best students. I had one that was a model, and she did their industry. I also had a student that was a stripper. So, you have competition."

I shot back, "Professor K., mark my words."

Then I reached in my purse where I had a spare pair of panties. I sprayed them with ATP, my perfume, which stands for "Assume The Position". I got up behind him and put them over his head so the crotch area was over his nose. Then I walked out. Had I known college was like hustling I would have finished ages ago.

LET ME FLOW:

Who You Want to Be

Who do I think I am?
Most folks would call me a hoe, tramp, or slut
Who do I think I am
I consider myself a good mother and wife

Some would call me arrogant, conceited, and
downright freaky
I consider myself sexually uninhibited and confident
Who do I think I am?
I am Maggie—the woman you wish you were

BTS:

I walked into the ladies' room, and who did I bump into? None other than Quida, who came up and hugged me.

"Maggie, how are you?" she asked.

I told her, "I am good now that I have turned my paper in to Professor Kindred."

"Maggie, I need your help," she stated. "I have a similar project as yours that was given to me by Professor Banks, who is also in charge of who stays here on track scholarship. I have to ace this course in order to keep my track scholarship. Can you please help me?"

LET ME FLOW:

What Should I Do?

Start back down to hoe alley
Or get on the trail of orgasm—forever
What should I do?
Help a friend
Or help myself
What should I do?

Enjoy having some uninhibited sex
Or start going to church
What should I do?

BTS:

As I came out of the fog, Quida had my arm gripped tightly.

I opened my eyes and replied, "Yes," not realizing what I actually agreed to.

Pause:

Maggie, what are you doing? You said you would change. How can I change if I'm still doing the same things? Or worse!

BTS:

After Quida tells me what her plans are and how we can go about accomplishing them, I tell her, "Freeze. I have never been a follower, and at this stage in my life, I am not going to start."

Agreeing, she stated, "Maggie, tell me when and where I need to be and what to do, and consider it done."

"Now we're talking, Quida. I need to find out some things about myself and Professor Kindred."

With a devilish look, Quida asked, "Professor Kindred? What do you want to know about him?"

"Folks like the Professor can always help you when you have a lil' dirt on them," I told her.

Looking puzzled, Quida said, "Dirt? What's that supposed to mean?"

"Quida, everybody in this life is hiding something. If I find out what the Professor is hiding, he will be my ally for life."

The light bulb moment for Quida occurred at that moment.

"Now I understand."

I decided I would give her the g-plan (game plan) the next day.

Quida walked me to my car and gave me a hug. "Thanks, Maggie. You're my girl for life."

LET ME FLOW:

What Am I Hiding?

What am I hiding?
I am always hiding something
It's either my feelings of emptiness
Or my need to have something I shouldn't

What am I hiding?
I have been this way for years
And never thought anything was wrong

What am I hiding?
I don't know
But guess what?
I don't want to find it

BTS:

I managed to duck Quida for two days. It's Saturday morning, and I realized my husband was still home. He usually worked on Saturdays, but he was still lying next to me. My sweetness always begged for attention. So, I just pulled off my panties and sat on his face.

PAUSE:

When your pussy is shaved, it is always ready and fresh. And when you have a good diet, it makes it that much better. I encourage drinking apple juice and cranberry juice. It will keep it tasty.

BTS:

He wakes up with two smiles; one from his lips and the other from my sweetness' lips. He began to devour it like he was eating pancakes with syrup. My moaning started.

PAUSE:

Ladies, ladies, ladies, moaning is encouragement. Never ever, and I mean NEVER, just lay there quietly while your man is attempting to please you. If you just lay there as if he is not doing anything, you can cancel Christmas. You have to feed his ego because it's hungry. Patronize him. He will get increasingly better, and in return, you will receive all the rewards of some terrific sex.

BTS:

So, as I fed his ego, he started doing some out-of-this-world moves. He does this move with his tongue that goes all the way up in my sweetness and hits my g-spot. He is simply amazing!

PAUSE:

So why am I still doing things that are not right?

LET ME FLOW:

Guilty Pleasures

Always searching for orgasms
Always searching for closeness
Guilty Pleasures
I don't know
I want to stop
Guilty Pleasures
It does not matter if you are single or married
I will put sweetness on you
Guilty Pleasures
I am guilty of always pleasing selfish me
That's really a Guilty Pleasure

BTS:

Now I am out of my daze. *This man is incredible!* His touch, his tenderness, his roughness when I need to be put in place. Damn, I love him. He stuck his tongue so far up in my sweetness that I swore he was licking my ovaries. After he finally took his tongue off my ovaries, I went to sleep with my thumb in my mouth.

LET ME FLOW:

Back in Love Again

My husband is the only man for me
From him always making sure I am okay
To him just tearing up my sweetness
Back in love again
To him taking care of all my financial needs
Back in love again
To the Mercedes that I drive
Our house on the Gold Coast
Back in love again
I am going to stop cheating
Because I'm back in love again

BTS:

Alas, the weekend ended, and in the blink of an eye, I was back in class. Quida approached me.

"Maggie, are you ready to start my assignment?"

I told her that I didn't think I could help her at the present time, or for that matter, any time in the near future.

"Maggie, what's going on with you?" she asked. "I thought we were girls. All of a sudden, you're telling me no. When you were doing your paper, I helped you. I even edited it for you. So, half of that grade is actually mine.

Maggie, I hate to do this, but if you don't help me, I'm going to tell Professor Kindred that your work is fraudulent, that you made up everything."

PAUSE:

Who is this lil' girl threatening? I do not take too kindly to threats. The last person to threaten me was Nichelle Mattis in the sixth grade. She wanted to open her big mouth and tell a boy I liked him. So, I put chewing gum in her hair, and she is still bald to this day.

BTS:

So, I pulled up real close to Quida and let her know, "Do not fuck with me by threatening me. I can make life rough for you."

She bucked back, "So, Maggie, is that a threat or a promise?"

Now she was leaning on me. She actually put just a touch of fear in me. *No one bucks back at Maggie.* So, I stated my case again.

In response, she told me, "Maggie, I am not asking you to meet me. I am telling you to be at the house by the coliseum at ten o'clock on Tuesday morning."

Then she walked away.

PAUSE:

Who the hell does this lil' girl think she is? No one threatens or walks away from Maggie!

BTS:

I sat there contemplating my situation. *What have I gotten myself into?* Quida could tell my professor. Even worse, what if she told my husband? I was faced with a reality check and also a gut-check because I felt I might have to hurt Quida.

PAUSE:

About six years ago, this girl, who was my friend at the time, sucked my boyfriend's dick, and I found out. I also found out that she had planned to hook up with him again. So, this is what I did. I went into the woods and got a batch of ants. I put them in a plastic bag. While we were in school, I turned the bag inside out into her panties. She ended up with a terrible infection. I think they named it after her. Or maybe they named it "Don't Mess With Maggie". Subtleness when you cross me is not my MO. It's worse than a Vicki and Dorian Lord fight on One Life to Live, or hell, a Crystal and Alexis fight on Dallas. This is real, no re-writes or characters coming back from the grave.

LET ME FLOW:

My Biggest Fear

My Biggest Fear
My husband finding out about me
My children finding out their mommy is a hoe

My Biggest Fear
Used to be just surviving
And having enough to eat
But now it's so much deeper

My Biggest Fear
What if someone is taping me
And I end up on TV?

My Biggest Fear
Is getting caught

BTS:

I snapped out of my daze, but was still thinking about how I could get her to stop pressing me without hurting her. There are three sides of Maggie–good, hoe, and killer. I recalled another time when a so-called friend did something I considered to be dirty. She used to be my husband's secretary, but when I found out she flashed her 46-DD tits at him, I flattened all the tires on her car and put sugar in her gas tank. That was the tip of the iceberg. Offering sex to my man could be volatile. I showed her just how much, too. I also called the DEA to her apartment. So, she no longer lives in that deluxe apartment in the high-rise in the sky. I think she lives in some homeless shelter. Identity theft and tampering is easier than tying your shoe. Messing with me is something you really need to think twice about!

Effortlessly, I came up with a plan so I could just be an observer. That way, I could document everything and give it to Professor Kindred. If I worked this the right way, I may end up being acknowledged in the book as a contributing author. Then I can write my own book. I always wanted to write a book. I just did not want everyone to know these were my escapades.

PAUSE:

Yes, I am a hoe and a freak. I am discreet about who knows. I guess I am bashful, maybe even ashamed. But who cares? I love it when I am doing it.

BTS:

I had a great idea. I would only tell Quida a piece of it. She just wanted to get her assignment completed. As always, Maggie had ulterior motives. I would not mind making some of my stories a play, movie, or whatever. It would give me pleasure in my spare time. So, since I already had my plan formulated in my wicked lil' genius brain, I went looking for Quida.

LET ME FLOW:

I Ain't Right

I plan to set Quida up
To satisfy my own self
I Ain't Right
I have no scruples, morals, or soul
I Ain't Right
If I was, I would not be doing this
But I Ain't Right

BTS:

As I was walking down the hallway of the Carter G. Woodson Building, Quida was running towards me. Once she reached me, I told her my plan and how we were going to have the time of our lives.

PAUSE:

I only plan to tell her half of what's going to happen. That's the problem with people nowadays. We run our mouths too much, and loose lips sink ships. My business is my business. Your business is mine, too, if it will help me in some way, shape, or fashion. Let's not get it twisted. If you are dumb enough to run your mouth, I'm going to capitalize from it. Most women tell too much of their business.

LIFE LESSON FOR WOMEN:

You cannot tell your girlfriends about all your skills or the skills of your man, but especially your skills. Because if she tells her man, he will be after you. Most times, sexual birds of a feather do not flock together. Let me break it down a little further for you. Your girlfriend does not do all the things you do sexually, and you don't do all the things she does. So, women, keep your mouth shut and keep your man!

Now, if your objective is to get her man, that's a horse of another color. Feed her like a starving animal and see how naïve she is running to tell her man what you do. It will probably go a little something-something like this:

Honey, you know such-in-such. I swear she will do let a man do anything to her. Umph! I'm glad I love myself more than that.

And honey will be thinking, *I can't wait to corner her ass at the next function and invite her on my next business trip! I wish you would let me do more to you!*

BTS:

"Maggie, what's the story?" Quida asked excitedly. "How are we going to pull this off?"

I told her, "We have to set up at another location."

"Why another place?" she asked.

I responded, "Because the things that will take place at the new location will completely blow your mind.

LET ME FLOW:

You Really Don't Know Me

I think you want to know me
But you are scared
I am so much like you
But also different from
What you are used to

You really don't know me
I am happy often, sad sometimes
And the other times you just don't know
My words are sometimes too real
And you don't know how to take me

You really don't know me
You want to have a relationship
But you are cautious of your own feelings
The way you feel for me was never planned
They just happened, and you think I am going to hurt you
You Really Don't Know Me

BTS:

I told Quida that I would give her the location and time later in the week.

While hugging me, she said, "Maggie, I didn't mean to threaten you the other day. We're supposed to be like sisters, and I threatened you. That's not love. That's hate. I will never do it again."

Now she had me apologizing. "And I'm sorry for refusing to help you."

We hugged again, and then I told her that we would hook up later.

LET ME FLOW:

My Friend

I don't know what friendship really is
I consider Quida my friend
But I considered others my friends earlier in life
So what really is a friend?
I have struggled with this since childhood
So really, can I call anyone my Friend?

LET ME FLOW:

Searching

What am I looking 4?
Who am I looking 4?
Why am I looking?
Searching?
I thought at this age
I would be settled
And know what I want
But here I am
Searching
Will I ever grow up?
Will I ever stop going down the path of destruction?
Or will I get stuck
Searching?
If you are alone
You can make this
Your home
If you want 2

BTS:

I told Quida that I would pick her up from her place at six-thirty on Friday, and she agreed.

PAUSE:

I have no idea on where I will be doing the experiment.

BTS:

So, I decided to call in some favors that are owed to me. I looked in my trunk and found two phone numbers. One was for Dank, and the other was for my old boyfriend/fuck partner. I called him Freight Train. His real name is Trent Dunlap, and he is now a stripper. I took the two numbers and left the house.

PAUSE:

Never call numbers from your house.

BTS:

I got in the car and drove down to the gas station on Euclid Street. That's where all the hustlers hung out making deals at the payphone before cell phones. It's one of the only payphones in this area outside of the Metro. So, I know it worked.

I wanted both of them there for the experiment. However, I knew if Freight Train came, I would eventually join in on the activities, and I just might get caught up. I really liked Freight Train. He was my boy when we were teenagers. We did everything together.

BEST FRIENDS:

I have had numerous friends, but my best friends are usually men. The reason for that is they share with me and teach me. I do the same with them, and I do not judge them. I actually taught Freight Train how to have oral sex with me. He asked one night if I could teach him, and I did. He taught me how to maneuver to take in a big dick. He was the first piece that size that I had. So, keep a good friend of the opposite sex. They are there to teach you.

BTS:

I make the call to Lil' Dank first. It rang once, twice, and when it got to the third ring, I hung up. Then I called back, hoping he had an answering machine. So, it rang twice, and then a woman answered. I stated who I was and then asked for Lil' Dank.

She stated, "He's not here. Would you like to leave a message?"

I say my name again and told her to let him know I would see him in class tomorrow.

She said, "Bye, sweetie." So, I assumed it was his momma.

Now I was really nervous and scared to call Freight Train.

PAUSE:

The one that got away. That's who Freight Train was to me. After all these years, I still think about him and all the fun we had. But, I was too young to understand what a real relationship was back then.

BTS:

I called the other number. Low and behold, on the first ring someone answered the phone.

"Hello," the voice responded.

I casually asked, "Is Trent Dunlap available?"

The caller responded in a deep baritone voice, "Trent is not available, but Freight Train is."

Just as I was about to hang up, I realized it is Trent.

"Hey, Maggie. How are you? I didn't think I would ever hear from you again.

"Hey Trent," I replied. "How did you know it was me?"

He said, "Maggie, I told you when I last saw you that you were the one for me. Everyone has that one person who they wish they could have had later in life."

PAUSE:

When Freight Train said that line, it took me back to the coliseum that night when I realized why they called him Freight Train and the feelings I had each time I thought of him.

I will not let him know, but he was my special one, also.

BTS:

"Why did you call?" Train asked.

I hesitated before replying, "I just wanted to know how you were doing."

Train laughed and responded, "Come on, Maggie. You were never good at lying. What do you need?"

"Train, this is a big favor," I told him. "If you can't do it, I will not be disappointed."

He said, "Come on, anything for you, Maggie."

"Okay, here it is. I need a place. I need you. And I need for one of my friends to be able to do an experiment."

He shouted, "What kind of experiment?" Then he said, "Can you meet me in thirty minutes on Shannon Place?"

I dropped the phone.

RECAP:

The tourist home on Shannon Place brought back memories of the first time Freight Train ran through me. It seemed like last week.

He talked to me and eased up on me. I eased back on him, and he stuffed that train in my sweetness. Every part of my body felt him, even my ears.

BTS:

I come back to my senses. I have no reason to want Freight again, but it keeps calling me.

LET ME FLOW:

It's Calling Me

I walk away
I run away
I close my ears

It's calling me
I change my thoughts
I can even go visit my mother

It's calling me
I hang out with my daughters
I do stuff for the PTA
Even do my classwork

It's calling me
I close my legs

I close my mouth
But it's still calling

You want to know what's calling me
It's sexual healings that's calling
Maggie, I want you back

BTS:

I returned to my senses. *Why do I constantly put myself through this?* I was tired, but it seemed I couldn't stop. I thought to myself, *After this is over, I need to start going to church.*

PAUSE:

For some reason, we think we cannot go to church until we have cleaned up all our sins. I once heard a reverend say that church was a hospital or repair shop. Some of us need an oil change and some need a complete overhaul. Well, I know Maggie needs a complete overhaul.

BTS:

Now I had to ponder how I could do this experiment and not get into trouble, then redeem myself and go back to church. My wicked mind went to work thinking everything through, actual shortcuts so I could fulfill everyone's missions. So, I went over to the tourist home on Shannon Place. I got there early hoping to beat Freight Train there so I could get my plan together.

PAUSE:

Being Maggie, I always have a plan. Good or bad, there is always a plan.

BTS:

I went to the front desk and get a room. They gave me keys. I found the room located on the back side of the building, which was perfect because I planned for there to be some hollering, screaming, and all sorts of nasty fulfilling things happening.

I also didn't need the manager calling the police, thinking someone was being hurt.

Once inside the room, I checked it out. Then I went back out to my car, went in the trunk, and took out a few things I had packed for the occasion, such as gels, lotions, anal ease, and condoms. Can't afford to get an STD.

I also had some restraints since I was now into bondage.

PAUSE:

Bondage—I love to tie men and women up. I also love to spank them and make them beg for my sweetness. Yes, what Maggie does is taboo!

BTS:

Once I got back to the room, I decided to take care of myself first. So, I pulled out my newest toy, a ten-inch dildo that's nice and chocolate. I named him The Dude.

PAUSE:

Ladies, you have to name all your toys.

BTS:

I talked to The Dude and told him, "You got a whole lot of work to do in a short time. I want to cum twice before everyone gets here."

The Dude didn't respond, of course.

So, I put it to work. I positioned my sweetness at the edge of the bed as The Dude went deeper and deeper inside me.

I had all sorts of thoughts going through my mind, from my girls to my husband to Easter Sunday.

Now that's a weird thought.

LET ME FLOW:

Easter Sunday

My husband
My daughters

I'm losing it
I am in a house
On the wrong side of town
I am married but continue to cheat

I am losing it
Sexual escapades with men and women

I am losing it
Guilt and deceit
Have become my friends

I know I have lost it

BTS:

I pulled The Dude out of my sweetness and put him in my mouth.

PAUSE:

I love the taste of me. If you tasted this good, you would love the taste of you, too.

BTS:

So, I started sucking on The Dude, getting my jaws ready for Freight Train later. I sucked and sucked the head. Then I deep-throat it, taking in about eight inches without gagging.

You know I've been practicing.

Then I take in the other two inches. With all ten inches in my mouth, my sweetness started flowing. I was cumming without any outside stimulation.

PAUSE:

I have always gotten my pleasure from pleasing others. So, when I give a man head, it's not about him. It's all about me—me having complete control over them. I could hurt them or please them. It's my choice. Most times, I please them.

BTS:

I put my hand in my sweetness and started doing counter-clockwise circles. Then I stood and went down to the floor. I turn The Dude on and sit on its head while simultaneously doing the counter-clockwise turns. I started screaming and shouting, "Damn! Yes! You motherfucker!"

I lowered myself down further on it. Now it was all the way in my ass. "Gotdamn! Gotdamn! Damn!"

But now, I was stuck because my legs wouldn't move. Then I heard a knock at the door.

"Maggie, are you alright?"

I could not identify the voice, but I needed help.

So, I said, "Please come in."

Low and behold, it was Freight Train in some biker shorts. His dick was bigger than his legs. I knew I needed to get out of there, but if I did that, I would be letting Quida and Freight Train down.

I am always trying to please others.

RECAP:

Since childhood, I have always had to please people, from my mother to my grandma to my brothers and sisters. I even pleased my peers. I have a problem telling people no.

BTS:

So, I sat there thinking, *What is my next move?* But how could I really think while still sitting on ten inches and stuck on the floor? When Freight entered, he stood there with a dumbfounded look and then rushed over to help me, pulling me up.

"Maggie, are you alright?"

I was embarrassed but turned on at the same time. It's like most women; we want to be rescued by a tall, dark, handsome man with a great "package". That's exactly what I had.

Once he picked me up, he was about to sit me down on the bed until I told him to lay me on my stomach. When he did, that's when he realized The Dude was in my ass. I asked him if he could pull it out.

"Maggie, girl, you're wild!" he said. "I didn't know you took it in the ass."

He pulled it out slowly, then turned it on and started fucking me with it. I'm no good. It was tearing me up, and I loved every minute of it. Then he did something I wasn't prepared for. He started talking real nasty to me as if he owned me, like I was the student and he was the teacher.

I was all so ready to learn.

He started again with his lesson, telling me how to position myself to avoid hurting myself and to get the best feelings I had ever felt. Then he told me to come and take what I wanted.

PAUSE:

As bold as Maggie is, I am usually not the aggressor.

BTS:

But, this time, he made me take the lead. Although scared, I did it anyway.

"Bring that big dick over here," I told him.

He positioned it closer to my face. I want to suck it, but my jaws weren't really up to it. Then my body began to react. The Dude was still in me working its magic. So, I came again.

Then the door opened. It was Quida and two other dudes.

I sat there soaking wet from my ass and totally embarrassed. Quida's mouth fell open. The two guys were just happy.

One dropped his pants right there and stated, "Let me join this party."

I looked at his face when he said that. He was not cute at all. Actually, he was butt-ugly. Then I looked down because now his pants were on the floor.

His dick was fighting to get out of his boxers. Since I don't do introductions, I pulled him towards me, and I was not disappointed.

It was about nine inches and as fat as a big dill pickle.

PAUSE:

As I said before, get them butt-ugly men and women. They will take you there. Their only job in life is to please you. I know it's not nice to say ugly folks should take care of you. But, it's true.

BTS:

As I pulled this dill pickle to me, I put both of my hands around it and started caressing it. I rubbed it up and down, down and up. Then, while everyone was watching, before I could get it close to my sweetness, he busted! I mean, it totally exploded!

PAUSE:

Men, young or old, LEARN DICK CONTROL!

BTS:

He came before he had my sweetness or even got one lick on his dick. So, of course, I was disappointed. But, it also brought me back to my senses.

While I stood there still butt naked, Quida started taking off her clothes. She had become so bold with her sexuality after hanging out with me.

PAUSE:

I created a sexual beast! I should be proud. But, I'm not. I am starting to grow a conscience.

LET ME FLOW:

Opening Up Pandora's Box

To someone who otherwise
Would have led a boring life
Letting all her inner demons
And outer freak
Develop in less than a month
Could it be I really am human
And not such a bad person

BTS:

Who was I fooling? My past had come back to haunt me.

RECAP:

I once saw my mother and one of her girlfriends with this man in our basement. They were taking turns on him, one of them riding his face while the other sucked him off. I was hiding behind the bar. I saw it all.

BTS:

I blocked that out so I wouldn't start crying and then threw myself back into the situation. I pulled Mr. Cum-Too-Quick back over to me. He was embarrassed. So, I soothed his mind by telling him that once he got his monster back up, I would take care of it. He smiled and immediately, it was back at attention.

PSA:

Women, if you don't learn anything else from Maggie, learn how to handle a man. As Maggie always does, she compliments a man at all times, which feeds his ego, which feeds his performance in bed and always leads to his checkbook, credit card, or wallet. Sometimes all three and even his car. Maybe even a new car or SUV for yourself. So, ladies, keep the compliments coming.

Let me throw this in for free. If you are married, you have to stay in compliment land. The reason most men cheat is because some other woman starts complimenting him and making him feel good about himself instead of chastising him and criticizing him. That's the same for women—she cheats because someone is paying attention to her. This is NEVER about sex.

BTS:

As I massaged Mr. Cum-Too-Quick's dick, it stuck up in the air. Quida was now standing by me, and I told her to take over. She did as instructed. Then I pulled Freight Train towards me and whispered in his ear while Quida started sucking on Mr. Cum-Too-Quick. I told Freight Train to shove his dick into Quida as far as he could.

"Maggie, that's going to hurt her," he told me.

I replied, "Freight, do what I say."

He said, "Maggie, you've changed. Why would you want me to hurt her? I didn't hurt you. I'm known to take my time.

PAUSE:

I am delirious now. Maggie is totally out of control.

BTS:

When Freight told me no, I was dumbfounded. *Who does he think he is? No one tells Maggie no.*

So, I told him again, "Shove it in," but he paid no attention to me.

PAUSE:

I know I have lost it now. Someone actually told me no. In all of my years that word has not been in my dictionary 'cause I never heard it.

BTS:

Mr. Cum-Too-Quick was pressing me for some of my sweetness. I just gave in, and he handled his business very well. I was actually enjoying it too much.

I could see Quida in La-La Land as the other dude licked down her back. I never even saw her take her clothes off. I guess I was in my own world, 'cause she was now butt naked with Freight Train standing over her. She was all smiles.

I was enjoying myself, as well. But, of course, I needed to be first with Freight Train since he was my first love. As much as I didn't want to admit, I really did love him.

LET ME FLOW:

What is Love?

Is it good sex?
Is it good fun?
Is it someone who cares?
What is Love?

Is it intimate?
Is it fulfilling?
Is it just a dream?
What is Love?

It could be all these things
'Cause I don't know
What is Love?

BTS:

Now back in Maggie mode, I needed to get with Freight Train and finish where we left off so many years ago. While Mr. Cum-Too-Quick was still working, I decided to make him cum even faster. I started contracting my sweetness' muscles. My muscles are so trained inside my sweetness that I can make the hardest dick cum in seconds. So, as the sweet muscles were put to work, Mr. Cum-Too-Quick let loose. He pulled out, and the condom was full. Excited, he reached for his pants, pulled out another condom, and yelled, "Part two!"

I said, "Freeze! There is no part two for you."

"Come on, girl," he said. "You know I'm the bomb. I fucked your brains out!"

LESSON:

Men, please, pretty please, let us sing your praises about your bedroom performance. If we do not, for real, you did not do the job. We were faking! And yes, men, we fake it so good that we make you believe you were great. You start buying us stuff as if we are enjoying you. All the time, it is for material or financial gain.

BTS:

It was time for me to quit the charade. Noticing that Quida was getting pleased in more ways than one, I decided it was time to get to Freight Train and then get back to my family. So, I called Freight over and told him exactly what I needed him to do for me.

PAUSE:

Ladies, the reason you cannot get pleased from your husband or boyfriend is because you assume he knows what you want. Most times, he doesn't even know what he wants. Sex is not taught. It's learned from doing.

Most of us, including myself, do not know what we want or what turns us on until we experience it. Let it be oral, penetration, touching, or just words. We don't know until we experience it for ourselves.

BTS:

So, I told Freight Train I wanted it fast and hard. I told him that I wanted to get on my knees on the floor. At first, he hesitated.

Then I said, "Come on, Freight. You know you want this as much as I do. Let's do it for old time's sake."

He started smiling.

I looked down at his dick, and it was even fatter than I remembered. But, it also looked like it was swollen. He slipped on a condom and it broke. He pulled out another and it broke, too. Then he pulled out another, and it also tore.

By now, I was no good. *Maybe I shouldn't be doing Freight Train,* I thought. *Is this some biblical sign? Or are these just some cheap condoms?*

Is it time for me to go to church?

What's happening?

Should I let him go in me raw?

No, I can't do that. Too many STD's floating around.

LET ME FLOW:

Maggie

Maggie, big dicks, and having fun
Has my fun come to an end?
Will my love for big dicks
Be the death of me

Can I just leave
And live a normal life
Like most wives and mothers

Why do I have to be
Caught up in mischief
Conflict and sexual innuendo

Why is what Maggie
Do
Always
Taboo

The End

Mr. Roarke
Feenin' Again

My Mind, My Soul, My Penis

My mind is teaching
My mind is learning
My mind sometimes has control
My mind is sometimes dangerous

My soul is healing
My soul is bleeding
Sometimes just because
My soul cares, my soul
Wants to stop hurting
My soul yearns for someone
To love me

My penis, well, my penis
Wants every hole it can have
Has a mind and soul of its own
Will conquer you just because
My penis is deadly
My penis will hurt you
My penis is so powerful
It's because you let it
That's why what I do is Taboo

RECAP:

*L*ast time I talked to you, I was sleeping in my condo in Top of the Hill, and someone was choking me. I was still weak from being shot earlier that week.

BTS:

The hands were still around my neck. I was losing consciousness. *Who could this be?* I put my hand up trying to stop them. My left arm was the one I got shot in, and the bullet was still there. Weak, I was about to completely black out. But before I did, I started praying:

Dear Heavenly Father,

I know I have not been the best person. But is this the way you want me to go? By the hands of someone else? I know I have done a good job of killing myself, but I am not ready to go. So, please, rescue me. I will change. I will change. In Jesus' name I pray.

I was completely gone now. I couldn't even breathe. This was the part that scared me.

OUTER BODY EXPERIENCE:

I was floating through the room and could see two people in my bedroom. I couldn't figure out who they were. But, I could tell there were a male and a female with their hands around my neck. I was gagging. Then I fell unconscious. They were smiling while killing me. I still couldn't figure out who they were. Then I started to see faces. *Damn, I know them.* But, I didn't understand why they would want to hurt me out of all the people who wanted a piece of Roarke. These two were the least likely that I thought would want to kill me.

LET ME FLOW:

Why?

Two people with their
Hands around my neck
I have lost consciousness
But I cannot figure out
Why

Yes, I have been rotten
To women and men
By sleeping with their
Sisters, wives, girlfriends
Even some of their mothers
Why

I told you I have no cut cards
So why didn't I see this happening?
I want to stay just a little while longer
Why

Should they let me survive?
Why

BTS:

I looked up and wondered why these two people were trying to kill me. Then the faces become clearer. I could clearly see Cicely and Joseph. I think someone must have told him about us. It was in the vault until I got shot. One of the fellas must have told him.

PAUSE:

The young lady that Joseph has a baby by, he thought he was the first one to hit it. I did her first on their prom night. She has been lying all these years to him, and he just found out.

BTS:

So now I understood why they would be mad. But, kill me? Come on.

LET ME FLOW:

Killing is Harsh

Last time someone said
They would kill me
It was Tessa's father

Killing is harsh
That was the first time
I used that line

But it seems like
Every time I turn around
Someone wants to kill me

Killing is harsh
Now I have been shot
And still have the bullet in my arm

Killing is harsh
At one time, everyone loved Mr. Roarke
Did what I said when I said it
Now everyone wants to kill me

Killing is harsh

BTS:

I didn't know if I was dead or just dreaming. I couldn't feel myself breathing. So, I was floating again, observing these two people doing all they could to choke me to death. *Now what am I supposed to do?* I knew I didn't deserve to be there. I had hurt so many souls, hearts, feelings, and just messed up some women's lives forever. Now, for some reason, I wanted this couple to have pity on me.

RECAP:

Mr. Roarke is what I am called. My birth name is Courtney Fitzgerald Edwards. An older woman at my job gave me the name Mr. Roarke because she said I made all her fantasies come true. However, the first name I was given was Lil' Game after my father, Big Game. He invented how to get women to do anything—good, bad, nasty, whatever! My father had control over all women except my mother.

I despised him as a child, but ran in his footsteps as an adult. Actually, I became worse because he controlled their bodies with his sexual prowess. I not only controlled their bodies, I controlled their thoughts, which is so much more power. By controlling their minds, I controlled their checkbooks, their cars, and even where they went.

PAUSE:

Mind control is the strongest control you can have over a person. It can even be deadly 'cause they always want to please who has control of their mind.

BREAKDOWN:

It's like you have an addiction that you cannot control and not knowing when you will ever get that control back. It's the worse when someone controls your every thought. To put it plainly, you are a puppet, and they have control of the strings. They keep pulling and manipulating them. Sometimes for the pleasure, sometimes for yours, and other times to harm you or have you harm or hurt someone else. Call me the Puppet Master!

BTS:

I was still unconscious, but my mind was floating on the ceiling. I was stuck in all the mess I had created in this life, all the hearts I had broken apart. For some strange reason, I felt that someone should have mercy on me.

PAUSE:

I had no mercy my whole life on others, besides my mother. No one was off limits. I did mothers, daughters, nieces, cousins, best friends, enemies, coworkers, waitresses, postal women, cashiers, secretaries, business owners, strippers, models, lawyers, doctors, babysitters, bank teller, singers, songwriters, schoolteachers. When I think of some more, I will tell you. But I am not bragging. As I have gotten older, I just get sad. So maybe I really need to leave this place. This song starts going through my head. It's a song that I only know a few words to and do not know the artist. It goes like this:

> *"I thought we'd live*
> *To see forever*
> *But forever has gone away*
> *It's so hard to say*
> *Goodbye to yesterday"*

Now I remember where I heard the song. It's from the movie Cooley High. That's the song they played when the main character Cochise got killed.

Could I be Cochise? If I am, where is Preach? That would have to be Dre. I stated years ago that Dre and I would never be like Cochise and Preach by fighting over a girl. But, here I am dying, and Dre is still living. He is nowhere to be found.

Like Florida Evans on Good Times, damn, damn, damn! What am I supposed to do? I guess I'm going to die. Will God intervene on my behalf? Please this is the ninth hour and I have no one else but you.

Dear God,
I want to stay a whole lot. Hopefully you feel the same. I know from going to church and Bible study that the devil can only do what you let him.

Dear God,
It's me begging again.

Dear God,
Will I survive or go away?
Dear God,
What are you going to do with me?

BTS:

I was still looking down. Will this nightmare ever end or am I dead? Am I going to die? I felt like I was submerged in some deep water. I was totally blacking out. I couldn't breathe.

LET ME EXPLAIN:

The commentator for the story as of this moment is unknown.

BTS:

Mr. Roarke blacked out completely. They wrapped his body in blankets and bed sheets. He was bleeding from his nose, and his face was bruised. While they were choking him, they smacked and punched him in the face.

They had him all wrapped up. The man picked up his head, and the woman picked up his feet. After they dragged him to the door, she looked out and checked to see if the coast was clear.

She closed the door really hard.

"What's wrong?" he asked.

She had a look of fear on her face.

"What's wrong?" he asked again.

She said, "That damn Dre is coming down the hallway."

Now they were both panicking, trying to get rid of the body. So, they locked the door and started pulling the body over to the balcony. They could hear the key in the door as they were trying to throw the body over the balcony.

When Dre opened the door, all hell broke loose. Dre came in hollering, "Roarke! Roarke! Roarke!"

They had the body in the air ready to throw him off the balcony.

Dre was still hollering, "Where the hell are you, Roarke?"

He heard the commotion outside and ran to the balcony. Realizing what was going on, he smacked Cicely simple. Then he knocked Joseph smooth out. Dre unwrapped the bed sheets and saw Roarke's bloody face. He lost it and started whipping Joseph's ass. Then he started kicking Cicely.

Suddenly, Roarke coughed up blood and cried, "Dre... Dre...Dre, help me."

Dre stopped kicking ass and went back to Roarke.

"Roarke, you're alive!"

THEN HE BREAKS DOWN INTO

We Boys for Life

No matter what
No matter when
We Boys for Life
Midnight or daylight
Rain, sleet, snow, hail
Or on the metro bus
We Boys for Life
No woman or money
Can come between us
'Cause
We Boys for Life
Dre

BTS:

Dre went to the phone to call the police. First, he tied up Cicely and Joseph with tape, socks, shoestrings, and bed sheets. He then picked up Roarke and put him on the couch. Roarke's nose would not stop bleeding, and he was still spitting up blood.

The police finally arrived. When they walked in and saw all the blood, they drew their guns. Dre had his hands in the air while he explained to the officers what had happened.

PAUSE:

You are never innocent when it comes to police and black men. So, growing up in the hood, we learned to assume the position, and Dre did just that. We know a whole lot of innocent black men that are no longer here because they did not assume the position. It's second nature, like breathing, for black men growing up in the hood.

BTS:

While foggy, I could make out in bits and pieces what happened. One of the officers was a fine, short, Spanish woman with a heavy accent. She could still get it, though.

Oh yeah, back to almost dying. The fine butch officer, who I could have brought back to the right team or at least signed her up for both teams, asked Dre what happened.

Dre explained what he knew, showing the officers the river of blood coming from my nose. He then showed them the trail of blood from the front door to the balcony.

The officer called the ambulance so they could transport me back to the hospital.

I begged Dre, "Don't let them put me back in there. I'm fine, just a little sore." Although, I knew my nose was broken, and my jaw was also sore."

Within minutes, the paramedics were in my face taking my blood pressure. I told them that I had just gotten out of the hospital. They asked me if I wanted to stay the night in the hospital for observation.

I told them, "No. Hopefully, y'all can give me some medicine and let me stay here and sleep."

LET ME FLOW:

I Gotta Hold On

I am feeling weak
Been feeling sick
I gotta hold on
People are trying to kill me
Bashed my face in
I gotta hold on
The odds are against me
But they have never
Been in my favor
I gotta hold on
I want to change
I will do things differently
I gotta hold on

BTS:

They checked all my vital signs and told me that I had a mild concussion, a broken nose, and maybe a fractured jaw. They said if I agreed to go the hospital or doctor the following day, they would give me some medicine to ease the pain for that night.

Dre and I agreed, and they gave Dre the medication and directions on how to administer them. Dre asked me if I was okay to walk. He sat me up in the chair and gave me the medicine, which knocked me out within minutes.

When I awoke, I was in an unfamiliar place. It was unfamiliar because I had not been there in a while. It was Dre's place in Marlbury Plaza on Good Hope Road.

After I got my senses back, I was okay. Dre's place had always been real comfortable. It was always very clean just like his truck. So, I was at peace for a minute.

Dre came into the room with a bowl of Oodles of Noodles and a big cup of Kool-Aid. Now I was really feeling at home.

He asked, "Roarke, can you walk and how do you feel?"

Before I answered...

LET ME FLOW:

Safe at Last

I am at Dre's place
Out of harm's way
Safe at last
No one is trying to kill me
No one is punching me
Safe at last
Finally, I can get some rest
Finally, I am not watching my back
Safe at last

BTS:

I told Dre that I was fine and appreciated all that he had done for me the last two weeks.

Dre broke down and said, "Damn, Roarke, we need to get back in church. We need to pray more. This is crazy. In one week, someone tries to kill you twice. Man, Roarke, we must be living wrong. Hey, when you are healthy, we're not only going back to church. I want to join the choir, deacon, and usher. I need constant time in the building."

"I agree, Dre. Let me get healthy first. Then we will come up with a plan together, 'cause this is going to be the hardest thing we both have done."

RECAP:

Dre is asking me to change with him. He is basically telling me to be a one-woman man, which is so hard for me. I have been a hoe for so long. Then when Tessa broke my heart, I lost my mind. How can I be with just one woman all the time? I have never seen a good marriage. I don't even know a lot of married folk.

BTS:

I told Dre, "Let's take our time with this. No need to rush."

Then he got bold and shouted, "Roarke, you get killed by yourself. I'm going to church and get me a relationship with God."

"Hold up, Dre. You don't have to get with God by going to church. God is in your heart, mind, and actions."

A classic Roarke mantra.

PAUSE:

I learned that by attending Sunday school as a child, then again in bible study as an adult.

BTS:

Dre said, "Okay, Roarke. Since you know so much about God, why did he let you get shot and why were those folks trying to throw you off the balcony, Mr. Gotdamn-Know-It-All!"

PAUSE:

Dre is pissed. He never hollers or curses at me.

BTS:

So, I said, "Dre, in the Bible, the Devil actually used to be in Heaven. God threw him out for acting foolishly while there. So, the Devil knows the word of God better than most folks. And, also from the Bible, God only allows the Devil to do what God needs to happen. The Devil asks permission to do the things he does and puts us in the positions we are in. Sometimes God grants him the authority. Other times he tells him no. So, Dre, this could have been a whole lot worse than it is now."

Dre said, "Roarke, how do you know this?"

My response was, "Dre, as you know my favorite thing to do is read."

He said, "Yeah?"

Then I said, "Dre, I read the Bible and all sorts of religious material. I hunger for knowledge, and lately, it's been knowledge of God. I am not a Bible quoter. From reading as much of the Bible as I have read these last years, I know its content very well."

Dre responded, "Roarke, I am totally speechless. You never cease to amaze me. So, Roarke, since you know all this stuff about God, Jesus, and the Bible, why do you act the way you do? You are a straight-up cruel fool. The only person you care about is your mother and sometimes me.

Knowing all you do about the Bible, how can you still be the same person?"

"Dre, let me sleep on that because I don't know. But, I promise when I wake up, I will answer."

Later the next morning, Dre came over and asked if I was okay. He then helped me to sit up.

"I'm fine," I told him.

After helping me up, he said, "Roarke, we need to go down to the police station so we can press charges on Cicely and Joseph for trying to kill you."

I responded, "Dre, this is where I am walking my Christian walk. I could press charges, which would result in jail time for both of them. But, the Bible tells you to forgive others and their sins. The Lord forgave me for all the nonsense I did to people. So, I have to grant them that same privilege."

Dre stood there with his mouth wide open looking astonished! I asked him if he is okay.

He said, "Yes, but this is not the Roarke I am used to. The Roarke I know would have not only pressed charges, but would have had some get-back, too. Code of the street, Roarke! I don't get it. They tried to kill you, and because you're not dead you don't want to press charges?"

LET'S GO BACK IN TIME:

Back in the early 80's, Dre and I got into a situation in Philly while visiting his cousin. These girls that we were dating lived on the bad side of town. It was the North Side. The building they lived in looked like the building the Evans family lived in on Good Times. The balconies were fenced. The elevators did not have lights and rarely worked. It was a bad neighborhood. But, these two sisters were FINE!

PAUSE:

For some reason, the finest girls are always from the projects. Let me describe them. Caramel complexion, perfectly round asses, pretty faces, and nice sized breasts. So, as I said—FINE!

AS I WAS SAYING:

After we came from one of the after-hour spots about one o'clock in the morning, some of the neighborhood guys came at Dre and me.

Dre said, "Roarke, it's six of them. Let's run and get my cousin and his folks and come back."

I said, "No, Dre, we got this."

By living in the hood for so many years myself, there were not too many things or people that scared me. For some reason, I was always a fool on my own. So, a fight with six dudes was right up my alley. Being the genius that I am, I saw some bricks, two beer bottles, and three big sticks like off a dining room table. They started punching at Dre and me. I gave Dre one of the table legs, and I grabbed two. We beat their asses so bad, they were crawling away from us. Then, I stepped on one of their knees and heard it snap. Then, I kicked him in the head. I don't play that shit. They don't know we from Barry Farms—Southeast, Washington, DC. It's just some shit I will never let happen. If you try to hurt my boy or me, you got problems. We did what we had to do.

BTS:

So, I told Dre that I am no longer that ruthless person that I used to be. But, I was still no sucker. You can't just push me around and then have the audacity to think I'm going to let it ride. I told Dre that I needed to get some more sleep. Then I would go see my mother.

After waking up, I wake Dre up and told him he could stay in while I went to see M.

He said, "Roarke, use your keys, and I will meet you in two hours."

I went into the bathroom to wash up and didn't even really see myself in the mirror. I was still weak and felt terrible. But, I really needed to go see my mother. So, I got myself together and limped out to the car. Before pulling off, I prayed:

"Please, God, let this be over. Let no one be outside waiting for me. Please, God, let me make it into M's house peacefully. Please, God, let me change, because I sure want to. Please, God, help me change. I want to be a better person. Please, God."

When I finally reached Dre's truck, I didn't remember which key was the right one. I hadn't driven Dre's truck in a while, and I had too many keys on my key chain.

PAUSE:

Dre and I had keys to each other's condos and cars in case we had to switch cars or condos due to jealous girls or husbands/boyfriends trying to get to us. Man law. Know the rules, baby!

BTS:

I start the truck, and on his stereo I hear an old Lou Rawls song called "I Go Crazy". It goes like this:

Hello girl.
It's been a while.
You would be glad to know
I learned how to laugh and smile.
Getting over you was hard,
But they say old lovers
Can be good friends.
I thought I would never see you again.

The hook is:
I go crazy when I look in your eyes.
I still go crazy.

Damn, now I was thinking about Tessa. I knew I needed to move on. I was trying to forget about her. Actually, I didn't even want her back. I was trying to convince myself. Now that I was driving, I felt kind of faint. But, I really needed to see M. Sometimes I think she is my key to God.

As I pulled up to the house, I saw M on the balcony watering her plants. I got out of the truck.

She hollered down, "Roarke, you okay?"

I said, "Yes, M. I need to tell you about last night."

I finally made it in the house and joined her on the balcony.

PAUSE:

I told you before my mother is a prophet.

BTS:

She started telling me what happened at my place last night.

She also said, "Roarke that is why I told you to stay here. But, remember there will be at least one more attempt on your life. You already survived three. My visions tell me there is one more. It does not tell me if you will survive."

She grabbed my hands and started praying and speaking in tongues. Then she kissed me and said, "Go home. I will call Dre and tell him to meet you there."

PAUSE:

This is freaking me out. I was just thinking that I needed to call Dre to tell him to meet me at my house.

BTS:

I went downstairs and into the truck. As I pulled off, I waved and blew the horn. Once I got up the street, who did I see? Priscilla. She waved me over. For some reason, she validated me.

RECAP:

Who is Priscilla? She is the ugly girl from my mother's street that burnt me with the tremendous blowjob. She is also the one that I used the trash bag in lieu of a rubber at my condo. I ran out of condoms and used a trash bag. I cut the bag to fit my dick and put rubber bands around it, and she still burnt me.

BTS:

So I pulled over and let her get in. For some reason, men need women to validate them.

BREAKDOWN:

We need them to let us know we still "Mack-Daddy" even when we're not. It's always some stupid women that will hold on to us even though we are no good. They are just happy to have a man. That's exactly why we do the things we do with no remorse. That's a history lesson on men. If you don't allow us to be, or at least feel like we are in control, then we are GONE! Sad to say, but just the nature of man makes him want to be a ruler. It's from prehistoric times. The man wants to be the lion, meaning King of the Jungle.

BTS:

As Priscilla got in the truck, she smiled, showing all those extra teeth. I would have loved for her to give me one of those tremendous blowjobs she was famous for. But, I was trying to change. Still, my dick wanted to stay the same.

PAUSE:

My dick has a mind of its own. Most times, it's doing stuff that I have no answer for, and the other times it's doing stuff I make it do. So, at all times, it's fucking—and that's a damn shame! But, somebody has to do it.

BTS:

I kept pondering whether I should get a blowjob from Priscilla or just go home. While we were in the truck, I asked her what she would like to do tonight.

She said, "Whatever you want to do."

PAUSE:

Ladies, make up your mind for yourself. Never say those words - whatever you want to do. We will run your life from then on.

BTS:

As much as I wanted to get a blowjob and do her, I decided against it. Instead, I made a U-turn and pulled back in front of Shipley Market on 23rd.

She asked, "Why are we back here?"

I told her that I had something I needed to do.

"Well okay," she responded. Then she went into her purse and wrote down her phone number, got out, and walked around to the driver's side to hand it to me. "Call me sometime," she said.

PAUSE:

Never make enemies. So, by not throwing her out of the car, I don't have to worry about her opening her mouth about us. So, fellas, if you respect them out of the bed, they will disrespect themselves in the bed. In other words, they will do anything you want them to do behind closed doors.

BTS:

I started to ride back towards my place. All these new thoughts were floating through my mind, and I couldn't deny them. I started sobbing uncontrollably.

LET ME FLOW:

I Know I Am Changed

I see a freak and
Don't get a blowjob or some pussy
I let her go
I know I am changed

I start to care about others
And I want to change
I know I am changed

My heart has been heavy lately
And it's because I don't
See things or people the same
I know I am changed

BTS:

I pulled over to the side of the road. I needed to get myself together. So, I prayed:

Hey God
It's me as usual
For some reason
I am calling you more

Hey God
Can this stop
I am tired weak and pitiful

Hey God

I finally got myself together and pulled back on to the street. I needed to get back to my place to meet Dre. Looking up, I saw a parking space in my building's lot. I pulled in, got out, and started walking towards the building. Candy called my name from a distance. Then she started saying, "Mr. Dick, Mr. Dick, can you help a lady out?"

PAUSE:

Women, please learn how to make your man feel like Mr. Big at all times. That was Candy's specialty. She always knew how to make me feel good about myself. Even if she was lying, she always said the right things. So, women, learn how to push your man's buttons.

BREAKDOWN:

Get in his head, and you will own his thoughts and know what makes him feel like Mr. Big.

BTS:

As I'm getting the bags out of the car, these thoughts raced through my mind. I don't know who was happier–her pants, her panties, or me. Candy had the most perfect ass, and she was bending over. It was totally irresistible. So, I touched it.

My, my, my, soft and tight at the same time.

"Roarke, don't start nothing you can't finish," she remarked.

"Is that a threat, Candy?"

"Mr. Dick, pull your dick out right now, right here in the parking lot."

"What?"

"Right here, right now."

Mind you, it's broad daylight at three o'clock on a Saturday. I did it anyway, though. She sucked so hard, it felt like her lips were a vacuum cleaner. I pulled away and pulled up my pants.

LET ME FLOW:

DAMN, DAMN, DAMN—OH MY!

That's all I can say!

BTS:

So, we went into the building.

Candy said, "Let's take the freight elevator so we don't have to wait."

I just followed with the bags. We got on the freight elevator. It went up two floors and stopped. Actually, it didn't stop on its own. Candy stopped it. She grabbed the bags out of my hands and put them on the floor. Then she started to do a striptease act, but she wasn't acting.

Remember, Candy used to be a stripper. So, the things she was doing were more than just sexy. They were downright sensual, erotic, exotic, and freaky. She had a freak like myself blushing. She was completely naked. Then, she put one leg up on the wall of the elevator and turned backwards. Her leg was up so far, I swear I could see her ovaries.

Then she said, "Roarke, get some of this pussy. It's all yours. I love you."

REECT:

I think I actually love Candy, also. She is the one female I respect and have never taken advantage of. I tell her my hopes, dreams, and wishes. I also share my fears with her. I spend a lot of time with her, and because we wanted to remain friends, we stopped sleeping with each other.

BTS:

"Stop, Candy. We really need to talk," I told her.

She said, "Roarke, I'm tired of being your friend. Make me your girlfriend or your fuck partner. I need you. I want you. I deserve you."

She does not need someone like me, I thought. *I'm rotten to the core. Hopefully, I can change.*

LET ME FLOW:

Rotten Roarke

An old girlfriend called me that
I always ran from the label

Rotten Roarke
He said how someone could love
Someone so rotten

Rotten Roarke
Can I get better?
I have tried
But seem to always fail

Rotten Roarke
Will this be my destiny?
To stay rotten
I hope not
I have lived up to the name

Rotten Roarke

BTS:

Candy put her clothes back on, and we finally got off the elevator. I opened the door, put my bags on the floor, and tried to leave, but Candy grabbed my face and put her tongue in my mouth. I started to cry. She opened her eyes and looked at me.

"Roarke, are you okay?"

I sat down and told her everything that was going on with me. We talked for hours after we put her food up. That night, I actually made love, I think, for the first time. We caressed and held each other for hours.

We did every sexual position possible. Candy is triple-jointed, so she was incredible. Ass in the air, pussy flowing with juices, and riding, Candy was the number one cowgirl in America. She rode my dick so many ways that I think I strained it. And she made me wear condoms. Each time I came, she put on a new one with her mouth. *I know I love her now.*

LET ME FLOW:

How Do You Define Love?

When you want to please them
Always want them happy
Go out of your way for them
How do you define love?
Make them your one and only mission
Make yourself secondary
Respect them and cater to them
How do you define love?
Your finances are spent on them
Your every thought is about them
That's how you define love

BTS:

We were lying in her bed exhausted, and for some reason, I was actually happy. I had not felt this way since Tessa and I were together.

Candy asked me, "Roarke, why are you smiling so hard? You're always so serious with a deep look on your face."

My response was, "I'm happy. I think I know what happiness is. I have been searching all my life and trying to get it via people, places, money, cars, women, and material things."

We sat straight up in the bed as I explained what real happiness is. "Real happiness is a relationship with a higher being. Mine is God. Yours may be Allah or Buddha. I cannot tell you who to worship, but God has been good to me."

Candy asked, "How did you get so close to God all of a sudden?"

I let her know that Dre and I had been going to church for a while, even before I got shot. I was brought up in the church. Like most folks, once I became a teenager, I stopped going and my mother started going more. She told me that she was always praying for me. I attended Catholic Church as a child with my father when they were doing services in Latin.

"So, Roarke, you really believe in Jesus, huh?"

I said, "Yes, Candy. In society, men are conditioned to act like we know everything, and it's all about our education or just male prowess that we know and do the things we do. But, now that I truly know Jesus, I know it has never been about me. Only reason I'm still here is because He has spared my life. I thank Him every day for sparing me. But, I know He needs me to do something. I just don't know what yet."

Candy said, "Explain that. God wants you to do something for Him? How does that work? He does something for you, you do something for Him?"

I told her to stop right there.

HERE IS THE BREAKDOWN:

The Bible states that God loves the sinner and not the sin. He still loves me, but He wants me to do better. The Bible also states, "He came so I can have life and have it more abundantly." There are scriptures in the Bible to back up everything I say. I have lied about enough things in my life. I don't lie on the Bible, God, or Jesus.

PAUSE:

I know I have changed just by me talking about the Bible, God, and Jesus. I have always talked about myself. I know I am evolving, and I like the new me.

BTS:

She then said, "Roarke, can we go to church together? I have not been since I was twelve, and you know I am a CME. I go Christmas, Mother's Day, and Easter."

I busted out laughing because I knew a whole lot of CME's. In fact, I used to be one. I told you Candy was easy to talk to. *I love this girl.*

PAUSE:

Women, let your guard down and become your man's best friend. He will reveal all his secrets, hopes, dreams, and desires. This is how Candy has Roarke wide open. From day one, she let her guard down and has been his closest confidant.

BTS:

We continued to discuss religion and agreed we would start going to church together and that we would just be honest with each other.

PAUSE:

Someone agrees to be honest with me? This is a first. I have always been the honest one. But no one has ever told me, "Let's be honest together." Not even Tessa.

BTS:

So I knew I had changed. We caressed and kissed the night away. I did not need any more penetration. I was happy just holding her. And I had never been this happy. It's like Candy completed me.

PAUSE:

Completion. That's a word I have never used. I did not think I even knew the meaning. I will try to explain with my own definition. Completion—having all you need mentally, spiritually, emotionally, and sometimes physically; not desiring anything extra. That's my version of completion.

BTS:

It was a different place for me. But, I felt safe and almost completely secure—almost. You can't feel completely secure until you are married, until you are completely attached to someone by the ring, ceremony, and commitment of marriage. That's my opinion.

We continued to talk and discuss if there was really a future for us. Candy started to reveal her true feelings for me.

"Roarke, what I really like about you is not the obvious. Yes, you're popular and have numerous things going on for you like owning your consulting firm, a car, a condo. You dress well and everyone loves you. And of course, having sex with you is totally a dream come true. But none of that does it for me.

"What I adore about you, Roarke, are your leadership skills. You run everybody you come in contact with—women and men, everybody from hustlers, businessmen, and hoes. That's the real turn-on for me. When you say it, people run to do it with no questions asked.

"Now, Roarke, that power is what makes me adore you. That's the power I have always had myself, but I never knew how to harness it or make it work for me in its full potential. You have mastered it. That's what I want. Together, we could be a powerful couple."

I started to smile and asked her if she was ready to take on being Mrs. Edwards.

"I know you're aware of the benefits. But, are you prepared to deal with the pitfalls that come with being with someone who's under a microscope 24/7? People watch my every move and sometimes follow me."

Candy responded, "I really do, Roarke. I'm sure I can handle everything that goes with being Mrs. Edwards."

LET ME FLOW:

Wifey

She wants to be my number one
My one and only
Wifey

I do really like her
Think I love her
Wifey
Always at my side
Forever have my back
Wifey

Was there when I was down
Actually picked me up
Will do anything for me
Even kill
Now that's a wife

BTS:

After that discussion, I didn't know what I should say to Candy. I wanted to commit fully, but even though I am my own man, there were two others missing from this decision. Those two were God and my mother. Now that I was talking to Him more, I tried to include Him in all of my decisions.

Also, my mother was the wisest human I knew. So, I always tried to have her in on my decisions. At one time in life, I made decisions with Dre. As I got older and wiser, I realized Dre, as well as the other fellas we ran with, waited on my every move before they would make one. That was a whole lot of undue pressure. Everyone was waiting for me to fail or succeed.

LET ME FLOW:

Reaching Down Inside

It's so hard sometimes
I don't have anything left
My resilience is steadily getting weaker
My know-how is leaving
My get up and go is almost gone
Dizzy sometimes, nervous sometimes
Decisions are never firm
I don't know if I have anything
To reach down inside to get

BTS:

I needed to go see my mother. When I tell Candy this, she said, "I would love to meet your mother, Roarke."

PAUSE:

The only women that get to meet my mother are women who I am dead serious about. Since I've been dating, the only one to meet her was Tessa. And I vowed to never let another woman hurt me. Also, I vowed never to let my mother almost hurt them.

125

RECAP:

After the breakup with Tessa, even though I was wrong, my mother really wanted to hurt Tessa because she hurt me. Yes, I am a momma's boy.

BTS:

Candy and I continued to enjoy each other. By her being triple-jointed, she did this move that had me totally fulfilled. The move was difficult to do. So, let me give you the most vivid version as possible.

DESCRIPTION:

She was completely naked. There was a chair in the corner by the window. She got on the chair and rolled up in a ball. When she opened up, her legs were hugging around the bottom half of the back of the chair. She told me to sit in the window so I could understand where I needed to be. I was totally confused. I didn't know what to do. The pussy was wide-open waiting for entry, but I didn't know how to get to it safely without spraining myself. So, I asked her.

PAUSE:

Fellas, don't be afraid to ask a woman if what you are doing to her is pleasing her. This is the only true way to total pleasure. Once she tells you what turns her on or off, you will know how to proceed. Also, ladies, learn your own bodies. Get some toy—vibrators, butt plugs, the bullet, or maybe the rabbit—and explore yourself. So, when you are asked or the man needs some help or assistance, you can tell or show him, which will lead to some terrific sex.

BTS:

Since I asked, she guided me into where she needed me. I'm so glad I asked. I was totally lost. She guided me into her by bracing me on the floor.

PAUSE:

Pull out your camera, pen, pad, and your imagination, and bring sturdy arms and legs.

BTS:

She told me to do a handstand and put my feet in the window, which I did. She grabbed one of my legs and pulled me closer to her. Then she positioned me to have me completely over top of her. So, here I was with my arms on the floor bracing myself, feet on the window to be steady.

Now, here's the fun part. I was actually over top of the pussy upside down. My adrenaline was running both ways into my dick and to my brain by being upside down. She guided my dick into her waiting pussy and gripped it with her muscles, starting to work me into a frenzy. I didn't feel like I could breathe. Then it happened. Let me explain.

While I was upside down, the blood flow was incredible. I couldn't cum. So, my thrusts became synchronized with hers. The motions we were doing together were actually blowing my mind. The blood flowing to my head was taking me to a new height. I was about to lose it. I could no longer hold myself up. I told Candy this, and she grabbed a hold of my body. Mind you, I was almost unconscious, fading quickly. The next thing I knew, I woke up in the bed.

LET ME FLOW:

Can It Be Any Better?

Can it be any better?
She makes me happy
She loves me
She is my everything

Can it be any better?
She cares when others leave
She is always that one
Her actions are always
Geared for my enjoyment

Can it be any better?
She shares in my thoughts
And wishes the best for me
Can it be any better?

BTS:

The next morning, I reached over, but no Candy. There was an aroma coming from the kitchen. So, I went to the bathroom and then snuck into the kitchen. Candy was standing at the stove wearing a French maid outfit, complete with thigh-high fishnet stockings, high heel shoes, and no panties.

I returned to the bedroom without her noticing I had been watching her. Back in the bed with my dick in my hand, I got some lubricant from the side of the bed and started to massage myself. I worked myself up to an orgasm with my eyes closed.

I couldn't wait for Candy to join me. Just the thought of her in that outfit made me need to get myself off even more. When I opened my eyes, Candy was standing right over me. She had put the food down and had her right nipple in her mouth with her hand inside her pussy. I was embarrassed and turned on at the same time. She had her eyes closed and was getting herself off. With the tip of her finger, she was playing with her clit like it was a yo-yo, fingering herself at the same time.

She looked like she had more than two hands.

PAUSE:

Men and women, learn how to please yourself first. Then you can teach your mate. But, if you do not know how to please you, how the hell do you want me to figure it out?

BTS:

While Candy was acting like an octopus, I put more lubricant on myself and went for round two. Candy fell into the bed, and we both continued working ourselves like it was the last piece of each other we would have for the rest of our lives.

PAUSE:

Men, in order to have a woman always saying you were the best, you have to act like it's your last piece before death. So, if you're going down on her, eat her so well each time that when she sees you years from now, she still *shakes. As for fucking or making love, make sure each time you enter her that you fulfill all her needs before you fulfill your own. Let me repeat that...**MAKE SURE YOU MAKE HER HAPPY BEFORE YOU TAKE CARE OF YOUR OWN SELFISH NEEDS**. This will guarantee you are always invited back.*

BTS:

We fell back asleep like we're not just sleeping together. We fell asleep in each other's arms like lovers. I imagined even further, like she was my wife.

We finally woke up about noon. I called my mother and asked her if she would be home for the next couple of hours. When she replied yes, I told her that I wanted her to meet someone very special to me.

My mother said, "If it's not Tessa, keep her to yourself. I told you when you were hurting that girl that she was the one for you. Now, all of a sudden, you tell me some BS about someone special. Roarke, the only person you care about is your DAMN SELF! BYE!"

After she hung up, I was left sitting there with tears rolling down my face. My mother had always been known to be brutally honest. Today, she took her tongue out on me. Yes, I deserved it, but I just didn't expect it.

LET ME FLOW:

My Mother

Brutally honest
Extraordinary love
Caring, giving, and passionate
Honest and true to her calling
Not only my mother,
But mother to the neighborhood
Our house was where you
Would find stability
All because of
My mother

BTS:

She was right about only caring about myself. But, I had started to grow now that I had been going to church and Bible study. I loved God, my mother, and then myself. That was my order. At one time, it was only myself. I also loved my brothers and sisters. I had been so consumed with loving myself that it was hard even comprehending the thought of loving someone like I loved myself. I had that feeling for Tessa. I think I had the same feelings for Candy. As for my mother, that was true love. I love her unconditionally, like the way Jesus loves us.

As I sat trying to regroup, Candy consoled me and asked, "Roarke, are you okay? Why are you crying?"

I told her that my mother said the only person I loved was myself. She held me tight and shared with me her deepest inner thoughts.

"Roarke, my mother always told me that. She not only told me I couldn't love anyone, but that I was evil and selfish. So, we are the same person, huh?"

I had no response. I guess because I agreed.

LET ME FLOW:

Just Like Me

How could there be two of me?
Struggles and thoughts the same
Mindset and actions
Very similar
Just like me
Always fifty steps ahead
Of all others
Never sleeping, always scheming
Just like me

BTS:

After thinking about us being just alike, I started to ponder, *Is that what I really want?* Being with someone who wanted the same things that I did could be fun. However, was this the one to marry? The thing about being with someone who acted just like me is that we would never be whole. We could never be whole because there were so many elements of life that I was lacking. If we were both missing the same things, we could never have a solid relationship. Another thing, I felt our relationship should have started differently, not just each other being the other's rebound guy and girl. Despite us having earth-shattering sex and orgasms that would make a submarine go off course, I felt something was missing from this relationship.

PROPHET:

Now I start to think about my mother, the prophet. Do I really care about anyone other than myself?

BTS:

I decided to go over to my mother's house.

After we showered and were putting our clothes on, Candy asked, "Are you sure you're ready to tell her?"

Before I could get my pants on, she was polishing my knob, and I was loving it. Candy loved oral sex more than penetration. Her reasoning was control. Oral sex gave you total control over the other party.

LET ME BREAK IT DOWN:

Oral sex is a science mastered by few. A whole lot of folks do it, but very few have mastered it. In order to be a master, the recipient of the services has to be totally hypnotized during and after the service is performed. Additionally, to be hypnotized, the recipient has to lose all sense of reality, such as being at work and unable to work or driving and not being able to remember directions.

Now you are the master, which means you can control them.

BTS:

She inhaled all parts of my dick. She had the dick in her mouth, and her tongue was rubbing my prostate. She went up and down on it, then pushed me on the bed and straddled me. She jumped right on it and started bucking up and down. I stopped her, though. I pushed her off and rolled out of bed.

She said, "Come back, Roarke."

"Candy put your clothes on," I responded. "We got to go see my mother."

We started back to putting on our clothes. Now I was mad because, as usual, I let my dick knock me off track.

Right before we left, I got nervous. My nerves were so bad that I was shaking.

Candy tried to reassure me. "Roarke, it's going to be fine. It's only your mother."

I responded, "Candy, you don't understand. I've been trying to please this woman since I was a child. She's a true Libra woman. She is fair to everyone else except me. She has always pushed me so hard to make me a better person, a good man, a Godly man. Heaven only knows why I am still trying to fulfill all of the things she wants of me. She also is harder on me than she is on all of my brothers and sisters. She rides me like there is no tomorrow, as if everything I do is bad."

REECTION:

Since childhood, my mother has been both my biggest cheerleader and my worst critic. She has always told me how brilliant I was and how brilliant I was going to be. On the other hand, her critical nature would always damper my spirit as if I was not good enough. But, I was good enough for the world, just not her.

BTS:

As we pulled up to her house, I was shaking like a leaf. Almost uncontrollable, it was getting to me. After parking, I got out and went to the other side of the car to open Candy's door. My mother was on the balcony watering her plants. She has a green thumb. Her plants were ten to fifteen years old and looked like small trees. She had names for all of them and even talked to them as if they were people.

I waved to her. "Hey, M."

She waved back and said, "Hi, Courtney."

I didn't know if her calling me Courtney was a good or bad thing.

She smiled as she said it. Then she said, "I see you have company. Come on in. I would love to meet her."

I flashed a look of confusion because M was never cordial with anyone. *What does she have up her sleeve?*

We went in, and I sat on the loveseat with Candy. M offered us something to drink. We both got lemonade. I excused myself and went to the bathroom. When I returned, Candy and M were laughing. M was sitting next to Candy with one of the old photo albums of me open on her lap. They were having a ball. So, I thought it was a good sign.

LET ME FLOW:

My Mother and My Future Wife

Laughing and talking
Smiling and grinning
Acting like they are old friends
My mother and my future wife
Hopefully they like each other
I know they both love me
My mother and my future wife
Mother and Candy
I love them both
My mother and my future wife

BTS:

I joined them and sat on the edge of the loveseat.

When my mother showed her pictures of Tessa, Candy said, "He liked that tall girl? She has an asymmetric hairdo." Then Candy busted out laughing.

That's when my mother lost it and told Candy that she needed to leave right now.

"Ms. Edwards, what did I do?" Candy asked.

M said, "You have no right to talk about Tessa. She is a nice girl. So, get the hell out!"

"But, Ms. Edwards..."

My mother cut her off. "Ms. Edwards, my ass! Young lady, get out of my house before I call you something else."

Then Candy bucked on my mother and said, "You don't have to talk to me like that."

At that moment, M smacked her so hard that her teeth rattle. I jumped between them. M swung and hit her again. Quickly, I grabbed M and walked her to the kitchen.

"Get that thang out of here and you leave, too!" she yelled.

Candy and I walked out of the house with our heads down. She was crying because my mother smacked her twice. I don't know why I was crying.

LET ME FLOW:

Lost

We get in the car
I am driving to nowhere
Lost
Tears are running down my face
So much that my pants are wet
My shirt looks like I just
Got out of the shower
Lost
My mind, heart, and feelings are
Lost
We are just riding in silence
Lost

BTS:

We finally got to Candy's house. I had been driving for three hours. Mind you, she only lived fifteen minutes from my mother's house. We just rode around without talking. Our tears were all dry. I couldn't even think straight. *How could M disrespect her like that? Don't she know I love Candy?*

My mother had always run my life. As much as I loved my mother, I had to stop her from ruining my life. I loved Candy, and I knew she was the one. *Why is my mother always interfering?*

Still totally speechless, we went up to her place. I grabbed my extra house key from off of Candy's dresser without her noticing and left her place.

LET ME FLOW:

Love Has Been Tough for Me

I can't find Mrs. Right
I am not even faithful to myself
Love has been tough for me
The person that I am now
And the person I thought I used to be
Are starting to look alike again
Love has been tough for me
When will I find true happiness?
Or will I ever find it?
Love has been tough for me

BTS:

I went over to my condo. The only way I knew how to get some peace in my life was to take a bath. So, I ran the bathwater, lit some candles and incense, and added bubble bath. Of course, I put on some really good music, songs about breaking up, such as "Make Up to Break Up", Lou

Rawls' "I go Crazy", "I Want to Go Outside in the Rain", and a whole lot of others.

There were so many bubbles, they were going up in the air and coming out of the tub. I lowered myself in the water, turned the music on, and drifted away from the present. I needed to get away. I closed my eyes and wondered how I got this way.

Why am I this way? Can I change? Do I like myself? Do I love myself? Do I belong here?

PAUSE:

Don't worry about Roarke hurting himself. That will never happen. He loves himself more than life itself.

BTS:

I sunk further and further into my zone. The water was just about over my head. I activated the jet setting so it could massage my back. I was loving this.

But what do I do about Candy? What do I do about my mother? What about the business? What about the New York office? What? What? What?

I soaked in the tub for hours contemplating my next move. When I finally got out, my chocolate skin was very wrinkled. I sat on my bed, looked in my mirror, and just wondered how I got here. I heard a voice say, "You need to get back in church."

I sat there like I didn't hear it, but the voice only got louder. "You need to stay in God's good grace."

By now, I am terrified. Then I realized it was just a radio advertisement for one of the gospel plays. For a minute, it had me. I was about to get on my knees and start repenting. When I knew Jesus was not coming for me at that moment, I started to lotion my body.

I put Shea butter all over me while enjoying myself. When I got to what most men call their manhood, which is their dick, I started massaging it. I have learned how to enjoy myself. I started rubbing it and talking to myself.

After about twenty minutes, it happened. My cum shot up so far that it ended up on my face. I pulled the sheets over me and fell into a deep trance, only to be greeted by those crazy dreams again.

My childhood was actually nice and fun. My parents had issues that you think will never bother you as a child. They don't bother you until you become an adult. Sometimes it can kill all your thoughts and dreams about a relationship.

RECAP:

Man. In my mind, the word "man" is so foreign to me because I have never known what it should mean. The male species that I knew—older, younger, and even my age—had no knowledge of this word, and truthfully, I don't either. I need to add more to this theory. But, I can't because I just don't know who, what, or why I am or even who I want to be.

BTS:

This dream was extremely difficult for me. My parents were not fighting this time. My mother was in the hospital, which was not unusual. She was born with a heart condition known as Rheumatic Fever, which is a hole in her heart.

So, I was no stranger to sitting in the hospital. That's really where I learned to pray.

I learned prayer because I always wanted her to get better, and I started talking to God each time I visited her there. She would get pretty sick once a year. That's when I really prayed.

However, in this particular dream, my mother did not make it. All the children were standing in the room, and she was dead. Tears were streaming down all of our cheeks, and none of us could catch our breaths. I tried to get wake myself from the dream, but I was stuck.

How could this be? The only woman who had unconditional love for me is gone? I must be crazy or drunk. I started to shake her.

"M, get up! M, get up! M, stop playing! Please get up!"

The other siblings were just standing there awestruck. We prayed, prayed, and prayed some more.

Now awake, I was sweating and crying, glad that the nightmare was over. I don't know what I would do without M.

MOMMA'S BOY:

Yes, I am a typical momma's boy, but she is so much more than a mother. She's my business partner, prophet, banker, and best friend. She is also the smartest person I have ever known, from her keen sense of business to just knowing people. No one could come between us.

BTS:

I started to think I needed to get over to M's house to apologize. Regardless of if I was right or wrong, I always needed to respect her. Heaven forbid she would pass away before I had a chance to get it right.

RECAP:

That's what happened when my father, Ronald, passed away. We were beefin' for years about something that really never happened. On Father's Day of the year he passed, we reconciled.

He died two months later at the tender age of forty-nine. I still had so many issues that were unresolved. But, I was happy when we reconciled. That's why when you go to funerals, you see folks trying to get into the casket at the church and when they are at the cemetery. It's because they have unresolved issues. Guilt can kill you.

BTS:

I got myself together and left out the complex to get my butt over to M's house. I finally got to her street, which seemed like an hour even though she only lived fifteen minutes from me. I have walked this path numerous times. But, today seemed different. I knocked on her door. M was sitting in the dining room.

She said, "Come on in, Courtney Edwards."

I went in and started to apologize, but she interrupted me.

"No need, son," she told me. "I should have warned you about Candy when you first told me that you were serious about her a while back."

I stood there dumbfounded.

"What do you mean? Do you know Candy?"

My mother said, "I don't know her personally, but when you first said her name, I had a vision and could actually see her face before you ever brought her over to the house.

"I did not want to say anything because, first of all, Courtney, I truly love you as my son. I really don't want to lose you again to a bullet, someone choking you, or some crazy girlfriend. You have been down all those pathways. The last time I told you about a young lady you were dating, you stopped speaking to me."

RECAP:

There were two incidents in my younger years when I was dating these redbones. Actually, one wasn't a redbone. She was a "proctor", which is a complexion that's higher than red. It's damn near white. She had some of the juiciest pussy ever, and M told me that she was not the one for me. I fought her on it, and low and behold, she was right. I am still finding out about friends of mine that she sexed.

Then there was the other redbone from Robinson Place. Not only was she a hustler's girlfriend, she was a one-night stand that I made my girlfriend. What was I thinking? I said it time and time again. Good pussy will make you do some crazy things!

BTS:

We sat in the house and talked for hours. When I finally, it was about one o'clock in the morning. As I drove up the street, who did I see? None other than Priscilla. She waved me over. She also had two girlfriends with her.

I pulled over. " What's up?"

She said, "Roarke, can you take us to 51 Liquor Store so we can get a drink?"

That's a late-night liquor store that stays open until three o'clock in the morning.

"Get in," I told them.

Her two friends were real nice. Ugly folks always hang with fine girls.

We engaged in some idle chitchat on our way to the store. Once we reached the store, Priscilla and one of the girls got out. The real fine one stayed with me in the car. When they went into the store, I pulled into a parking space.

When she got in the front passenger seat, I didn't know what to think. I didn't know her. But, of course, being Mr. Roarke, I wouldn't have minded knowing her. Especially since I needed to get out of the relationship I was in with Candy. Also, new pussy was always good.

She started talking about college and her plans for the future, which was odd because the women that I have met in the past only talk about what they can do sexually. So, this was actually a turn-on to me.

PAUSE:

Men and women, get into the mind. Everything else will come with it. Let us fall for your brain first. Then all the sex, money, cars, and credit cards will be second nature for us to give you access to them.

BTS:

I asked her name, and she responded, "Christian Kady."

"Oh, really?" I said. "Why do you feel the need to tell me your full name?"

She replied, "Because I would like to know yours."

I said, "I don't usually give out that information."

Then she said, "I am the exception. So let's hear your name."

For some reason, I told her Courtney Fitzgerald Edwards. She laughed and said, "We actually know each other."

I responded, "We do?"

"Courtney, you interviewed me a few years ago when I was going to Howard University. I interviewed for an internship with your company. But you didn't hire me."

My mouth was now wide open.

"What's wrong, Mr. Edwards? Cat got your tongue?"

RECAP:

When I first started my consulting firm, I hired my interns from Howard University. Dre and I also had sex with all of them. We hired them partially because they were fine. Christian was really fine. So, I don't know what happened with her. I don't know why Dre or I did not choose her. But hell, we don't know why we do half the things we do.

BTS:

After we got that out of the way, Christian stated, "I would love to see if we can form some type of partnership with P.F. & Associates and my marketing firm."

"So you are into marketing and advertisement?" I asked.

"Yes. My minor is English. My major was marketing. I have a Master's in Business Management."

"Wow! I'm impressed!"

Before we could finish our conversation, Priscilla and her other girlfriend returned. I said to myself, *Damn, damn, damn!* I was really feeling the conversation with Christian Kady.

Once they got in the car, Priscilla said, "Roarke, can I go home with you tonight? Wait. Let me reword that. Roarke, can all three of us go home with you tonight?"

Then Christian said, "Courtney, I will not be going home with you tonight." She pulled out her business card and handed it to me. "Call me on Monday. I don't get down like that."

PAUSE:

My dick is on the gas pedal. She is refusing to sleep with me the first night, and I am loving it. All my life, women have slept with me the first night, except Tessa. She made me wait a whole year. Man, Tessa was special. She always did things differently. She made me appreciate her.

BTS:

After coming out of the fog, I told Priscilla I was going home alone.

"So you don't want a threesome with us?" she responded.

"Priscilla, I've changed since the last time we were together." It had been about a year ago.

"So, Mr. Roarke is turning down some pussy, huh?" she replied, starting to get mad.

146

PAUSE:

Never let a woman get mad at you at any time because they are the most vindictive people. They can make life unbearable.

BTS:

I tried to put out Priscilla's fire, but it only grew.

"So I'm not good enough for you anymore, Roarke? Is that what you are saying?"

I said, "No, that's not it. I have really changed."

She started calling me names.

"No-good motherfucker, you think you the shit! That's why I burnt your ass. I tried to burn your dick off!"

Now S.E. Roarke kicked in. "You ugly, bug-looking bitch!"

We were going word for word. Then the bitch climbed over the seat and grabbed the steering wheel. I slowed down, but not before she got her arm stuck in the steering wheel. We were going over the curb and down the hill on Suitland Parkway. I had lost total control of the vehicle. Everyone was hollering, including me. We were airborne now.

PAUSE:

Only thing I could think of is my mother, the prophet, saying someone will try to kill you again and I am not sure if you will make it this time.

BTS:

The car plunged down the embankment. I wanted to start praying, but the only thing that came to mind were the words I wanted to say to Candy after finding out how much of a whore she was. And here it is:

LET ME FLOW:

I Don't Love You Anymore

My mind and heart was yours
My every thought was about you
I don't love you anymore

It was always about
What I could do to further
Your agenda
I don't love you anymore

You chastised me when I
Didn't agree with you
And did not return calls
When things did not go your way
I don't love you anymore!

Then I sunk into prayer
Lord, if it's your will, I am ready to come home.
In Jesus' name I pray
Amen

The End

In Remembrance

Much love and R.I.P., Lil' Benny. You were the best that ever did it. Thanks for coming to the taping of the Taboo talk show. Your spirit will forever live in us. LISTEN, CAT IN THE HAT.

Thank You

My thank you is a little different this time around. This piece of work drained me emotionally. I had to relive some unpleasant pieces of my life and bare my soul, which bought up some open wounds. Taboo IV was actually part of my healing process.

My first thank you is to my friend, business partner, prayer warrior and all-out love of my life—God. Thanks for keeping me together on this journey.

Now, let me take care of the humans that helped. The Queen of my castle, blood in my veins, the wall that holds me up—my wife Judy. I have heard it said before. Behind every strong man there is a woman holding him up. Let me take it a step further. Some days, I was on her back. Thanks for loving me.

Special love to my wonderful children—Kayla and Rodney. Kayla, Daddy loves you always. Rodney, be good today and every day. Take care of our favorite girls, Mommy and Kayla. Love you for who you are becoming.

Troy "Ghost Host" Rawlings, my friend, mentor, prayer partner, and just THAT DUDE, thanks for always pushing me. It's your time to shine. L.A., here he comes!

Shout out to Barry Farms. That's my hometown! Mad love to all the GO-GO bands; you are the soundtrack to my LIFE, especially Rare Essence and Junkyard Band.

Darell Barnes, Lisa Grey, Keith and Keno Davis, thanks for all you have done for the tour and just mad love whenever I am in B-more.

K. Lowery Moore, what can I say? You have become one of my best friends, from books to happy hour to just someone who I can vent to and with. You are a terrific author. Check out her website klowerymoore.vpweb.com for her great books.

John Gibbs, a true friend and great author. His books are *Who Knew It Was Broken* and *Bound by Unlocked Chains*. Visit him at www.whoknewitwasbroken.com.

Candice Simmons, a young lady who was amazing in our first meeting eight years ago. Now she is a phenom. World, she is the truth—writing, producing, filmmaking. She does it all, and I am so proud of her.

Tonya Frederick, I LOVE YOU MUCH. We are the best of friends, and yes, we are crazy together

Emily Henry (www.Emhenry.com) is my friend, co-host, and just an all-around good person.

Michelle Coles-Johnson—my friend, my editor, and my conscience. Thanks! Love you!

Sandra Harris, a great writer and the author of *The Party* and *The After Party*.

Ronda Rountree (www.rondarountree.com), a wonderful friend and dynamic author.

Yewande Seymour, through the brightest days and darkest nights you have been there. Love me some Yoruba. You are the best. Thanks for all the editing you have done to make this book a BESTSELLER.

Jessica Tilles, my good friend and wonderful author. Thanks for always encouraging me with your words. (www.jessicatilles.com)

J. Tremble, author of *Secrets of a Housewife* and *Secrets and more Secrets*. My road dawg from Stone Soul Picnic 'til this day.

Keira Smith, who would have thought you could write like you do. Thanks for your constant encouragement. Even when others have left, you kept on plugging away. You came in a season when I was just wondering. Thanks for pushing me back to my destiny. LOVE YA!

Treasure Blue, author of *Harlem Girl Lost* and *Street Girl Named Desire*. You're still a beast!

Kimberly K. Parker, President and CEO of Writing Momma Publishing, LLC (www.writingmomma.com). This past summer, her company published three books for young authors ages nine to nineteen! This fall, she will host "Write On!", which is an eight-week writing program for youth. She is currently looking for a few young writers who want to participate. Visit www.writingmomma.com for more information. Kimberly is a ghostwriter, author, and blogger who lives in Maryland with her husband and three children.

Lonnie Spry, author of *How Do I Go On* and *Speak Now...or Hold Your Piece*. (www.lonniespry.com) This brotha is FIRE!

Kwame Alexander, *Do The Write Thing*—This brother is awesome. His book is a must-have for all authors.

Michelle Donnelly, you are so special to me. Thanks for always pushing *TABOO*. Thanks to Kevin Brown and all the barbers at Classic Kutz at 23rd and Alabama Avenues in S.E.

Vera Kholheim Yancey, thanks for all your encouragement from the first day I met you at L'Enfant Plaza. You have been an angel.

My barbers and friends, Darryl Wade, Dre, and Ron's Cut Master.

Paula Childs, thanks for always making me feel big. You are a true friend.

Thanks to all the security guards at GSA and the cleaning crew. The Black Tiger Motorcycle Club, thanks for the love.

I extend much thanks to the folks who have been to the Taboo Talk Shows at the various locations and also to Cleveland Spears, the program director for www.im4radio.com, for believing in the Taboo Talk Show.

Tyi Flood, what can I say? Love you.

Gary Batman Green and family for always looking out for a brother from the Big Chair.

Shout out to my family—Marsha, Ruth, Robyn, Ronda, Rocky, Kristin, Maurice, Pete, Melvin, Brandon, Ryan, Michael, Christopher, Brian, Adrianne, Elaine, and Trey.

The angels watching over me—Rojena, Bumbry, and Robert Harrison.

My partners from day one—Melinda Robinson (www.motherhoodlove.com) World, she is preaching! T.T. Bridgeman—(www.ttbridgeman.com) *Poundcake for Sweetpea* and *Changing my Shoes*. Also Pastor Erline Stewart.

Shannell Davis, my friend, buddy, and shoulder to cry on, may God continue to bless your family and your business wwwprocurevis.com, the best placement service around.

One of my best friends, Shayla Jordan Carvelous. DC Bookman, thanks for all the love. Tiah, the Book Diva, you're the best.

Kelvin Lassiter, may the force be with you. You're the reason Book One is short. You taught me never to give them too much.

Thanks for all the inspiration from the many fans on the road. You know who you are. And the special folks that reappeared and disappeared through this journey.

If I forgot anybody, charge it to my head and not my heart, because it's that human in me that forgets. And guess what? I am just that—a human.

Thank You,
Yonder

Email: yondertaboo@gmail.com
Facebook - Yonder Harrison

This is a sample of the poems that will be in my upcoming book of poetry tentatively titled *EYE WONDER*. Hope you enjoy.

I Look Up

It's her
Chocolate and breathtaking
Fine in all the right places
Lips glistening
Eyes seductive
Looking at my spirit
Her soul gentle
Her soul seeping
Out her blouse
Her inner beauty
Equal to her outer beauty
Could this be?
Finally, I don't want to
Conquer her; just please her
I thought everything
I do was taboo
But somehow
This is too
Mr. Taboo loves you!

Never Forget

Changed my mind
Changed my ways
Changed my walk
Never forget
What you have done for me
Gave me insight
Gave me wisdom
Healed my heart
Never forget
Straighten my back
Changed my lust to love
Strengthen my character
So I could be respected
Never forget
Loved me so much
That I started
Loving myself
Never forget

Time, Place

It's your time
It's your place
It's your mission

It is your time to grow
It is your place to own
It is your mission to build

It's your time to enhance
It's your place to help others
It's your mission to do good

It's your time to live your mission
It's your place to get ready for the future
It's your mission that you do this now

It Broke My Heart

I've been a fool
Crying is not something I do often
Every time I think of her
I get teary-eyed
If it is not love
Why do I feel like this?
Please, Lord, get her out of
My Mind

Our Job

Most of us
Don't like our jobs
We get anxiety attacks
And are sleepless each night
Thinking about
Our job

We talk about it
We are mad at it
We despise it
Our Job

We never make enough money
And even if we do
We still can't stand
Our Job
So why do we put up with our job?

Saved

People have their view and model
Of who and what they consider saved

Saved is a state of my mind,
Which God and you have talked about and agreed on

It's not what society
Your friends, family members, or
Even your pastor has a say so in

As I said, it's an agreement
Between you and God

So, for all,
We judge what saved is on another
Ask God about yourself
Are You Saved?

Days Like This

Some days I want to let go
Life can be so hard
Insecurity is frustrating
Not knowing can be even
More frustrating

When and if you do find you
It scares you even more
Those days are spent
Wondering and dreaming

Days like this
You just pray

Do I Ever Cross Your Mind?

Makes me wonder
Days spent talking
Getting to know each other
Do I ever cross your mind?

Pray for you to be
The right one for me
Do I ever cross your mind?

Thinking and talking about you
Do I ever cross your mind?

In town or out of the country
Do I ever cross your mind?
Have you ever thought of calling?
And stopping to see me
Do I ever cross your mind?

Stay with Me

Don't leave
Let's just talk
Let me give you a massage
And cook you dinner

Stay with me
Let's express our thoughts on politics
Through children
To the judicial system

Stay with me
I will treat you like
The queen you are
Put you on your
Throne and praise
You all the while

Stay with me

8 Days and 20 Minutes

Nothing can stop how I feel
Nothing looks the same
Nothing tastes the same

8 days and 20 minutes
Me without you
Damn, I am miserable
Heartache and stressed out

8 days and 20 minutes
I thought I saw you
So I followed the car
When I got up to it
It wasn't you

8 days and 20 minutes
I am getting visions and
Seeing things that are not there

8 days and 20 minutes

Secret Service

It pleases me to slowly spread
The stories of her never-ending chocolate legs
From last eternity to next forever
It pleases me to look her square in the circles of her
Smiling windows and softly tell her
"I enjoy you" and we can turn everything off but the stars
So my eyes can adore you
Well-dressed in nothing but the skin with which God has
Adorned you
Smooth water, dark and rich from the sun's kiss
It pleases me to kiss everywhere the sun missed
Sculpted from the softest ebony
I expressly expressively appreciate…you
From your elaborate hairdo's to your 172 pairs of shoes
You take care of you
And that makes me want to take care of you
It pleases me to pay for your manicures and your
pedicures
Whatever your body requires to keep you in style
And in shape
To keep the smile on your face
And whenever your days or nights aren't as great
It is my pleasure to try to alleviate every woe and care
Roses everywhere, toes in the air
Soft moans in my ear, I hear you

New fresh like a breath of morning air in heaven
And I don't know how you get your hair smelling like
melon, mangos, and pears
But to me that just makes your whole body edible
From your temples at your temple
I am already ready to dine on you
Slowly pour white wine on you
Sip the sweet from your navel
I'm a hungry lion and you are my pride
I eat from your table
The nape of your neck, the shape of your breasts
The grace of your gestures, the taste of your nectar
You bend like a flower, you sleep like the moon
So soft and warm your skin feels like June
Your back like the Nile river, legs like waterfalls
You walk like light rain; in fact, you don't walk at all
You cascade into a dream, I lay you down like a queen
Who works hard for her title
It pleases me to please you
And to serve you is delightful
So now, don't speak, I bow at your feet
And place a perfect kiss in worship of your goddess
You are worth it to me, you have earned it to me
Every nerve is an ocean and every curve is a "C"
I submerge all of me deep into you
All into you, fall into you
Feel me, feel you, treat you how I see you
Feed you, eat you, squeeze you, release you
I please you because I need to; it pleases me to please you

KOMPLEX - Author of SECRET SERVICE

What manner of writer is he? Komplex aka Kom is a legend in process. He functions as a rare blend of genius-- a cross between Langston Hughes and Mos Def. Kom never ceases to amaze many; he is a poet and writer, hip-hop artist, published author and seasoned actor. His accolades include consecutive season performances on BET Lyric Café (2008 and 2009), and works aired on VH1 Soul and MTVU. His works received reviews in *The Source Magazine* (May 2009, pg. 88). He has also appeared in web TV shows, feature-length films, and theatrical productions. Kom has toured the U.S. extensively as a "celebrated" Spoken Word Artist who is considered by his fans and colleagues to be one of the best in the nation at his craft.